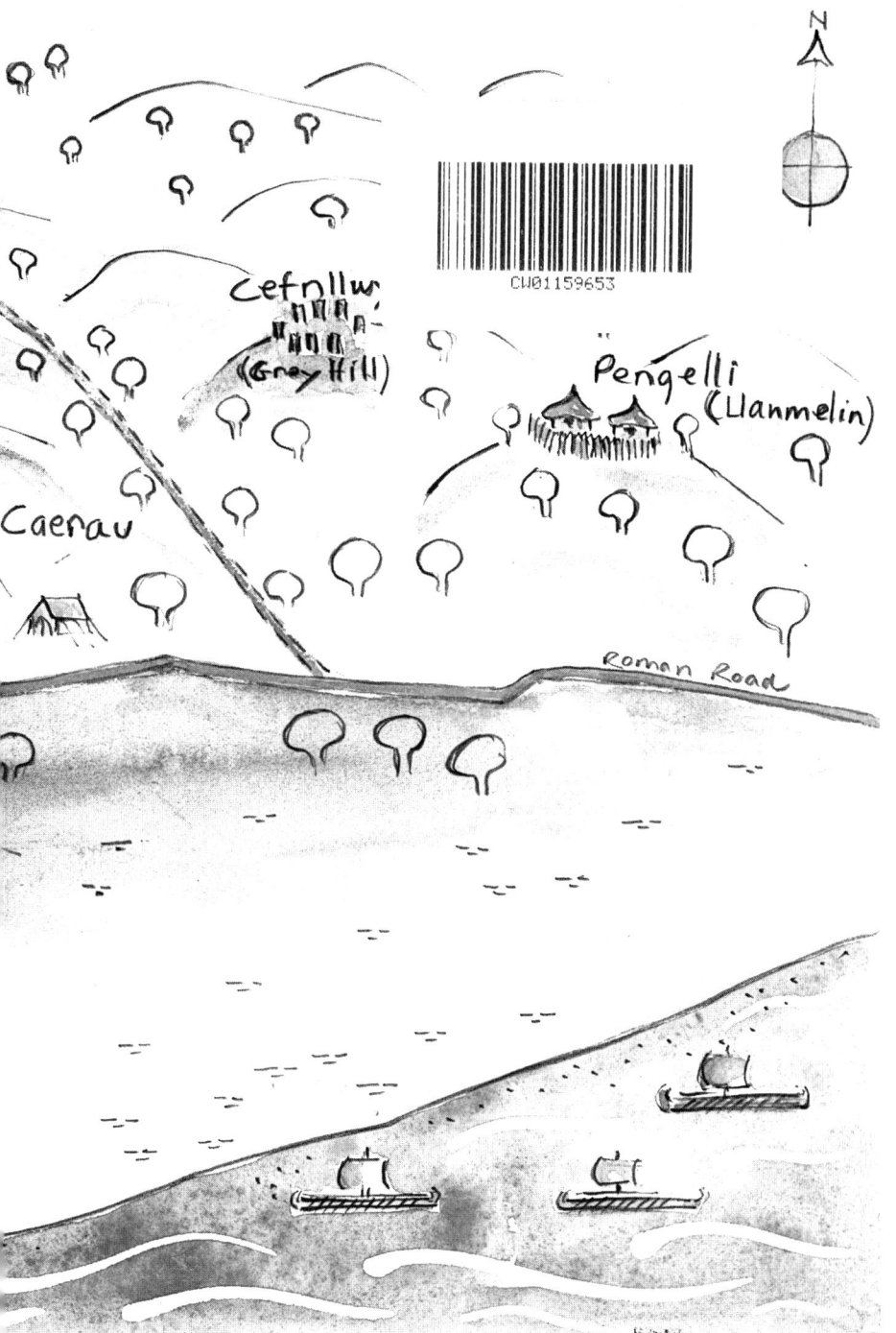

RHIANNON'S WAY

RHIANNON'S WAY

Margaret Isaac

Illustrations
Angela Hoppe Kingston

APECS PRESS CAERLEON

Published by
APECS Press
Caerleon
Wales UK

© Margaret Isaac 2002

Editing, design and typesetting by
APECS Press Caerleon

ISBN 0 9537267 8 9

All rights reserved.
No part of this work may be reproduced or stored
in an information retrieval system
(other than short excerpts for purposes of review)
without the express permission of the Publishers given in writing.

Margaret Isaac has asserted her right
under the Copyright, Design and Patents Act 1988
to be identified as author of this work.

Produced by Keith Brown & Sons Ltd, Cowbridge

By the same author

Tales of Gold
Stories of Caves, Gold and Magic

Nia and the Magic of the Lake
The story of a growing friendship between a boy and a girl
set against the backdrop of the legend of Llyn-y-Fan Fach

Sir Gawain and the Green Knight
A free translation for contemporary readers of
a Christmas tale of long ago

Teaching Story in the Primary School (1)
(Language resources for Key Stage 1 based on the story
'The Owl Who Was Afraid of the Dark' by Jill Tomlinson).

Language Learning through Story (2)
(Language resources for Key Stages 2 and 3 based on the story
'Nia and the Magic of the Lake' by Margaret Isaac).

Language Learning through Story (3)
(Language resources for Key Stages 2 and 3 based on the story
'Sir Gawain and the Green Knight' by Margaret Isaac).

Forthcoming publications

A Strange Birthday
A story about a little boy who is asthmatic and who wants to
spend his fifth birthday at home rather than in hospital

Tall Tales of Twm Sion Cati
In Tudor times, Wales was a land of poverty and persecution. Twm Sion
Cati was a famous Welsh outlaw, master of disguise, who outwitted the
enemy and carried out many daring deeds to help his people.

Teaching Story in the Primary School (4)
(Language Resources for Key Stages 2 and 3 based on the story
'Rhiannon's Way' by Margaret Isaac)

Welsh language translations of all publications

CONTENTS

Foreword	ix
Introduction	xi
PERILOUS TIMES	1
BETRAYAL	19
RHIANNON'S GIFT	31
RHIANNON IN DANGER	39
THE ROMAN CAMP	45
FRIENDS AND ENEMIES	55
TREACHERY IN THE ENEMY CAMP	77
CARADOG IN DANGER	89
HYWEL'S STRATEGY	101
VICTORY AND CELEBRATION	109
The Story of Rhiannon From The Mabinogion (as told by Brychan in the Great Hall at Pengelli)	117
Pronunciation of Names of Locations and Characters	127
The Silurians at Pengelli	128
The Romans at Brynpwca	129

FOREWORD

When the Romans attacked Britain, the Roman general, Agricola, declared that his soldiers had never faced more fierce enemies anywhere in the world than the Celts in Wales who fought with true courage and gallantry. In Rhiannon's Way, Margaret Isaac gives a unique picture of interaction between the Romans and the Celts in Wales seen through the eyes of two young friends, Rhiannon and Brychan.

Rhiannon, the heroine of the book gives the reader a fascinating view of Celtic life, depicting the warmth, liveliness and skill of her tribe, the Silures as they resourcefully get the better of the Romans. It is a refreshing change for the Romans to be the underdogs to the local population! The story has universal appeal as we sympathise with brave individuals who struggle against great adversity.

Careful research of Celtic life is evident. By her skilful use of language, the author has written an exciting, authentic story that makes the events come alive and holds the reader spellbound.

As in previous publications, Angela Hoppe Kingston has complemented and enhanced the descriptive quality of the text with delicately painted and evocative illustrations.

This enthralling book illustrates a key part of Wales' past. Margaret Isaac in Rhiannon's Way has produced writing that will captivate the interest of the young and the not-so-young.

Christine Loveland
Head of Classics
St. John's College
St. Mellons, Cardiff

INTRODUCTION

MUCH has been written about the Romans and the way in which they conquered and 'civilised' a large part of the modern world. When contemplating writing a story about Wales in Roman times, it seemed appropriate to consider this foreign invasion from the perspective of a people who had lived in their country for thousands of years. They were faced with a hostile and disciplined force, determined to conquer and assimilate the people into an alien way of life.

So I asked myself what it must have been like to be a Celt confronting the power and strength of a Roman Legion. Furthermore, I wondered how successful the Romans really were in defeating the Celtic people living in Wales at that time? In seeking the answers to these questions, I researched the history of the Celts in Wales in the first century A.D. and made some surprising discoveries.

I found that there was an extensive network of hill forts covering Wales. It seemed to me that here were the homes of an invisible people who had been forgotten by time. I found an interesting people, inventive and self-sufficient, lovers of music, art and poetry. I found a spiritual people with a strong sense of law and order. I found amazingly clever horsemen and women, ferocious and brave in battle. I found a people with a strong sense of family. Above all, I found men and women who were passionate and proud of their Celtic identity.

And so I have written my story from the point of view of the families whom I imagined lived in the hill fort located at Llanmelin near Caerwent. I have called this hill fort Pengelli.

I hope that I have breathed life into the people I have created, and conveyed some of the characteristics of the Silurian Celts who fought long and hard to preserve their way of life. They were eventually conquered by the Roman might. Or were they? The Romans left Wales in 410 A.D. leaving behind a people who had absorbed their cruelty and barbarism and adopted some of their ways. They continued to enjoy the Roman road systems and Roman central heating. But I believe that their innate spiritualism and Celtic identity remained untarnished.

I am indebted to the staff of the Roman Legionary Museum Caerleon, the National Museum Cardiff, The Museum of Welsh Life, Saint Fagans and CADW Welsh Historic Monuments, Cardiff for their help and advice while researching and writing this book.

Margaret Isaac

PERILOUS TIMES

Rhiannon's father Caradog is captured by the Romans and she decides to rescue him.

RHIANNON sat on her pony straining her eyes towards the woodlands in the East. As she sat motionless at the edge of the cool dark wood, the sound of a lark came from the deep ferns. She knew it was Brychan, she did not move. Then, purposefully, she turned the pony's head in the direction of the birdsong. Its hooves were bound with sacking so it made no noise.

Rhiannon pushed deeper into the ferns, then dismounted. The bitter smell of the ferns was comforting, the fronds felt soft and cool. She burrowed down and waited. Llwyd, her pony, quietly cropped the grass by her side. He looked at her, his liquid brown eyes eloquent. Then he turned and moved silently towards the waiting form lying hidden in the undergrowth.

Wordlessly, Rhiannon followed and wriggled through the ferns to lie by Brychan's side, he put his fingers on his lips. They listened and watched as a group of Roman soldiers marched along the track through the meadowland beneath them. The two friends watched until they were out of sight, then sat up and stretched themselves.

'I got your message,' said Brychan.

'My father has been captured by the Romans,' she said, 'we must do something.'

Rhiannon instinctively touched the brooch that fastened her cloak. It was an almost complete circle of bronze, with a triskele pattern on the two flattened ends. The Silurians believed the triskele was a magic sign that would protect them from harm. It was shaped like three curved arms joined at the middle.

She remembered when her father Caradog had given her the brooch. He had been away from

Perilous Times

home for two weeks, and Rhiannon knew without being told that he had been engaged in one of the many dangerous skirmishes with the invading Roman legions. He rarely talked about the fighting, but when he returned home and played games with Owain or laughed at Rhiannon's tales of her madcap escapades, he forgot the grim battles and was once more the kind, cheerful father Rhiannon loved.

Caradog was the leader of the Silurian tribe of Pengelli. He had a wife called Branwen and three children, Rhiannon, aged twelve, Gweneira, eight and Owain who was three.

3

Rhiannon's Way

They lived in the big house next to the Great Hall in Pengelli. Penarddun, Caradog's mother and Bryn, Branwen's father lived with them. Caradog's father, Eurion, had died fighting against the Romans.

Caradog was 28 years old and had fought many fierce battles defending his people from the incoming Roman invaders. He loved all his children but he had a very special relationship with his eldest daughter Rhiannon. He loved to listen to her talking about the days she spent with her friends.

'Yesterday we camped in the woods. Brychan and Gweneira climbed trees looking for red kites' nests, but I don't like climbing trees,' she said.

'Did they find any nests?' asked her father.

'They found a beautiful thrush's nest in a bramble bush.' Rhiannon's head was bent forward. She was making a daisy chain. Her thick, braided hair fell and covered her face.

'The nest was well hidden,' she continued, 'It was in a small bush, and Brychan pulled aside the prickly thorns so that I could have a better look. It was the same shape as the bowl I use when I eat my stew, and the birds had used lots of thin grass and straw and mud. They are so clever. I leaned over to peep inside, and there were four small eggs. They looked so fragile and were such pretty colours! I can't describe it really, they were sort of mottled greeny-bluey-grey with browny-black speckles. Brychan pointed to the two parent birds sitting not far away. They were anxious in case we did something to their eggs!'

'And did you?' asked her father.

'No, we were on our way down to the stream. You know, the one where you showed me the trout in the water, and I found newts.' Rhiannon looked up at her father and dropped the daisy chain. She was thinking about her expedition.

'We made up our minds to stay in our camp until morning, so we decided to have fish for supper. We went to the stream, with Gweneira, and we managed to catch three beautiful fat trout.'

'You've been learning a lot since I've been away,' her father looked at his daughter with a mixture of fondness and something like regret. 'You are getting quite grown up, camping, catching fish. Did you make a good fire to cook them?'

'Oh, yes,' said Rhiannon, 'Brychan is very good at building fires, he found plenty of wood, and we all cooked the fish together. They tasted wonderful. Brychan's mother had given him some bread, so we ate that as well.'

'And slept like logs no doubt,' laughed her father.

'Well, Gweneira giggled a lot,' admitted Rhiannon, 'and we had to keep telling her to shut up.'

'When we woke in the morning, we saddled up, and raced to the stables, Llwyd got there first, he always does.'

Her face flushed when she mentioned Llwyd. Her mother had given him to her for her tenth birthday. She remembered her birthday morning. Her mother took her down to the field with Gweneira and Owain. Llwyd was standing in the field, Rhiannon caught her breath. He was a lovely bay-coloured pony. His coat was fine and soft and shining. He had a thick dark mane and tail, a very pretty head with tiny pointed ears and large luminous eyes. He had a white flash from his forehead to his nose.

Rhiannon walked across to him slowly and carefully, but her heart was racing. She did not want

to frighten him. She put her hand to his nose and rubbed it gently talking to him all the time.

'Hello my beauty,' she whispered. 'Where do you come from?'

His ears twitched upright and he gave a little whicker as she kissed the end of his nose. He pushed his nose against her in a friendly trustful way and Rhiannon rubbed it gently.

'I won't have to take him back then,' laughed her mother, 'I can see that you two are going to get on fine.'

'He is the very best thing that has ever happened to me,' Rhiannon said passionately. 'I never ever want to lose him.'

Llwyd pushed his nose under her arm and gave another whinny, his ears pricked forward as he looked at his young mistress with fine intelligent eyes.

'I think he is trying to tell you that he is as happy as you are,' said her mother.

Rhiannon's happiest times were when she was with Rhidian in the stables. She usually groomed Llwyd after they had been out riding. She started at the pony's head, as Rhidian had taught her, whispering in his ear, telling him tales about the wonderful journeys they would make together. She loved combing and brushing his mane and tail and his beautiful coat until it gleamed a deep glossy red gold.

Rhidian was Caradog's brother. He lived near the stables with his wife Cigfa. He was 22 years old and she was 21. They had no children.

Rhidian was one of the most important people in Pengelli. He was a skilled craftsman and made the most beautiful gold, silver and copper jewellery, like the brooch given to Rhiannon by her father.

Most of the people of Pengelli wore Rhidian's jewellery round their necks, in their hair or on their arms or wrists. They also used cooking pots he made for them, in which they cooked their broths and stews.

Rhidian had learned his craft from his father, Eurion. As well as making jewellery and cooking pots, Rhidian made spearheads, scabbards, daggers, horse bits, harness mounts, and chariot rings.

Rhidian's nephews and nieces loved to help him with his work, and he was quite happy to give them tasks about the stables and the horses. He noticed that one of his nephews, Rhys, was particularly skilled at metal craft and he hoped that one day he would follow in his uncle's footsteps.

On one occasion, Caradog and Rhiannon were riding together through the woods and down to the stream. They dismounted and sat by the side of the stream. They watched a dipper, diving, swimming and running along the bottom of the stream looking for fish. Llwyd and Eiddgar, Caradog's dark chestnut horse, quietly cropped the grass nearby.

'I think, father,' she said, 'that Llwyd is very special.'

'I know he is very special to you,' said her father.

'No, I don't just mean that. He is special to me, that is true of course, but there is something more.' She hesitated. She did not know how to go on.

'He seems to have some sort of sixth sense.' She watched as the dipper rose to the surface of the water, a fish in its mouth. She went on.

'One day, I was out riding Llwyd alone. He stumbled and fell to his knees. He had caught his foot in a tangled creeper lying across the path. I was pitched forward and felt my collar bone crack. I don't know why, but something compelled me to whisper, "Quick, tell Brychan." I must have slipped into unconsciousness and woke up back at home in Pengelli. Brychan and mother were there and Meirion was bending over me binding my sore neck. Brychan told me that Llwyd had found him and guided him to me!'

'Perhaps you imagine too much,' said her father, but his face was serious.

'I expect you're right,' she said, although she did not sound convinced.

Father and daughter sat in a companionable silence. Rhiannon imagined the wind blowing through her hair as she rode her beloved Llwyd through the woods across the ridge to Cefnllwyd.

Caradog was deep in his own thoughts, pondering on his daughter's words. At last, he stirred and placed his hands inside the folds of his cloak. He drew out a mirror and gave it to his daughter.

'A lady gave me this present for you,' he said. 'Look after it, because it is very special.'

She looked at her father's gift. It was a bronze, oblong mirror with a twisted handle. Tendril-like swathes of basketry patterns decorated the back and the polished copper on the front reflected Rhiannon's girlish face with its braided plaits falling onto her shoulders. As Rhiannon looked into the mirror, she fancied her braids moved and changed shape of their own accord, until tiny horses' heads appeared to interweave with the coils of her hair.

Perplexed and a little troubled, she put the mirror into her lap, turning the copper face down so that she could no longer see the strange images.

'Where did you get it, father?' she asked.

'It was very curious,' he replied, as he watched her inspecting his gift. 'We were celebrating a victory with some people of the Demetae. I met a woman from that tribe and I told her about you, my beautiful daughter. She was the wife of a goldsmith of their people, and she gave me the mirror. She said her husband had made it for her, that it was a very special gift. She said it protected whoever owned it from harm. I thought she was being a bit fanciful but I didn't want to offend her. Her husband had died in battle, and she was still grieving. We had become friends and she wanted you to have it.' He paused.

'I've kept it until now. She seemed a strange woman, and she didn't want anyone else to know about where the mirror came from. She said telling anyone else may take away some of its magic powers.'

Her father smiled. 'I don't really believe her, but it is a lovely mirror.'

Rhiannon said nothing, but she thought of the reflection she had seen in the mirror, of the tiny horses' heads in the braids of her hair. She wondered if her father was too cynical about the woman's words.

Caradog's face grew hard.

'While I was there, I learned of what had happened to the holy men at Mona, and the terrible things the Romans had done to Boudicca and her daughters. They are barbarous enemies and we must drive them from our shores for ever.'

His voice was passionate. He looked again at his daughter, then turned his eyes once more to the busy bird life of the river, but his eyes had a faraway look, beyond the swirling grey waters.

Rhiannon looked at her father as he relaxed by the side of the river. He had a habit of twisting the gold ring on the second finger of his right hand when he sat and talked.

He was a very tall man, almost two metres in height and fighting fit. His thick, curling fair hair reached his shoulders. He wore a long tunic of linen cloth clasped round the middle with a splendid gold belt. A gold armlet encircled his right arm.

She remembered when she had helped Branwen to weave and dye the cloth for his trousers, they had created a special pattern and colours just for him. Caradog's thick cloak lay on the grass by his side. The brooch that fastened his cloak was S-shaped and made of bronze. The straight, plain pin of the brooch was attached to an elaborately carved fibula in the shape of a double-headed sword.

Rhiannon looked at the torc round her father's neck. This was a very special gift given to him by his father, Eurion before he died. It formed an almost complete circle and looked like a coiled golden rope with two golden pearls at the ends. The round-headed terminals were linked to the rope with entwined spiral patterns. Lines snaked out over the golden spheres, looping and winding round hidden birds perched on branches of trees and horses' heads interweaving with the elaborate curved patterns. She hoped it would protect him now as she thought of her father's determination to drive the Romans away from his land. She suddenly felt very afraid, for she loved him with all her heart, and missed him sorely when he left home to fight the Roman invaders.

She touched his arm. 'You know I will always try to make you proud of me,' she said.

He gave her his warm lovely smile, touched her hand lightly in reply and stood up. Brushing the grass from his clothes, he picked up his cloak and swung it over his shoulders. Rhiannon too, got up with a sigh and they both returned to their horses, mounted and rode home in silence.

Rhiannon sat on her bed and drew out the mirror. Her reflection stared back at her from the burnished copper, then the picture shifted and instead of her own face, she saw a beautiful woman dressed in gold riding a magnificent white horse. Then the woman disappeared, and the horse changed into a shabby-looking donkey. Tied against the back of the beast, slumped on a mud floor, lay a man sick and in rags. Rhiannon's stomach turned over when she recognised that the man was her father! She quickly turned the mirror over so that she could no longer see the disturbing picture in its shining copper face. But she could not resist taking another peep. She picked it up and turned the copper face towards her once more. She saw her own perplexed face staring back at her.

What did it mean? Could she have imagined the mystifying pictures she had just seen?

She put the mirror away, but she thought of her father's words:

'She seemed a strange woman, and she didn't want anyone else to know about where the mirror came from. She said telling anyone else may take away its magic. She said it protected whoever owned it from harm.'

Rhiannon slept little that night. The images she had seen in her father's gift haunted her. The woman riding her beautiful white horse must be her namesake, the great Rhiannon of the story told by the bards. Why had she seen that image in the burnished copper? Was the terrible picture of her father tied miserably to the back of a donkey some horrendous warning that he was in danger of his life? If so, what could she do about it?

Rhiannon's Way

When Rhiannon finally rose from bed, her father had gone.

Caradog usually left home without warning. Rhiannon would get up one morning and he would be gone. She always thought that she would never see her handsome, loving father again and thought her heart would break.

Her mother would go about her daily duties tight-lipped, as if she did not care. But Rhiannon cared, she cared desperately. When her father left home, her world fell apart.

But it was never quite as bad as she expected. 'He'll be back,' her mother would say, and it seemed that her mother was right, because he did come back - until now. Rhiannon's uncle, Hywel, had given her the message and she had sent to Brychan to meet her above the Great Water.

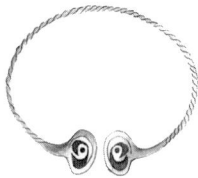

BETRAYAL

Rhiannon recounts the tale of the battle to Brychan They hide outside the Roman camp and find that her father has been betrayed and captured.

AND so it was that Rhiannon lay in the ferns with her friend, looking out across the water to Abona. It was their secret meeting-place.

Rhiannon turned over and lay on her back in the ferns. She looked up and watched the clouds scudding across the blue sky.

'Hywel told me last night.'

She thought of how Hywel, Caradog's brother, had sought her in the night. She had been sleeping fitfully, thinking of her father as she lay on her own comfortable straw bed. She had heard a scratching sound outside and had slipped quietly out into the night.

Hywel was covered in blood and grime as he recounted the tale to the young girl.

'Our scouts informed us that a large group of Romans were leaving the Brynpwca fort, marching towards Coed-y-Caerau. We hid in the hillside, watching, until we saw them stop and begin to set up their marching camp. Then we attacked.'

As Hywel had told Rhiannon the story, his face had become animated.

'The soldiers had formed a wall of shields with javelins sticking out from them at all angles. They were protecting the ones behind while they dug in to make their camp. We hurled stones down on them until they began to break ranks, then we charged down, swinging our huge swords, cutting down many of the soldiers, even their leaders. I saw Caradog and Rhodri urging their chariot into the middle of the Roman lines, fighting like wild boars, as they spurred the horses into the thick of the battle.

Then, we were surprised by cavalry soldiers bearing down suddenly on our left. Caradog turned his horses skilfully to meet the onslaught, but I saw the chariot turn over, and I thought I saw them fall beneath the horses' hooves. I tried to reach them but more Romans began to attack from the right. I swear they seemed to know that we were waiting to ambush them. We were forced to retreat.' Hywel hesitated. 'I hid until it was safe to go back and search for them. There was no sign of Caradog, only the chariot crushed and broken and the horses barely alive. Rhodri was beneath the chariot, dead.'

'Was Eiddgar one of the horses?' asked Rhiannon. 'Is he dead too?'

'We had to put him out of his misery,' Hywel said gently.

He knew how passionate Rhiannon was about horses, but he was also thinking of Rhodri's wife, his own sister Arianwen, now a widow, and of her three children Rhys, Pryderi and baby Chwerthin.

As if she had guessed his thoughts Rhiannon whispered, 'have you told Aunt Arianwen and my cousins?' She began to weep.

'I think Caradog may have been taken prisoner.'

Rhiannon had covered her face. Her shoulders began to shake. Hywel looked at her anxiously, and put his arms round her to comfort her.

She raised a tearstained face, 'I want to help you to find him,' she sobbed.

'I know you do,' said Hywel, 'you are a brave girl, and I will be expecting you to help me as soon as I have made plans. I will have to lead the Silurians now, while Caradog is missing, and Emyr and I will be working out a way to find out where he is, and how to rescue him.'

'I know you will,' said Rhiannon.'

She touched the brooch pinning her cloak and the pictures she had seen in the mirror came back to her, the woman Rhiannon on the white horse. Somehow the thought of the woman gave Rhiannon courage. She stood up. Whatever happened, she would try to rescue her father, she would have to be brave and try to make him proud of her.

'I must go and dress,' she said, and turned and re-entered the hut.

Betrayal

When she had finished recounting Hywel's story to Brychan, they sat for a while in silence on the hillside looking across at the great water. Rhiannon was thinking of a way to help in the rescue of her father.

'We know that they were at Coed-y-Caerau,' she said, 'they may be moving back to the Brynpwca fort. We need to make our way to the marching camp and get as near as we can to try to find out what has happened to my father.' She went on, 'It would be better if we waited until nightfall. We can easily hide from the Romans, they don't know their way around Pengelli and Cefnllwyd as well as we do.'

Brychan nodded his agreement, and as the two friends continued to lie in the ferns, they looked up at the blue sky, watching the drifting clouds. Butterflies fluttered around them as insects buzzed and birds sang. It was late afternoon.

It was difficult to believe that they were facing the prospect of spying on a fierce and cruel enemy.

'I'm glad you're coming with me,' said Rhiannon.

'You know I'll always help you if I can,' said Brychan, 'but I'm not sure that we will be able to do much to help your father. They have probably taken him prisoner to interrogate him.' He hesitated, he was a brave young man but he was more cautious than Rhiannon and feared for her safety. 'I have heard terrifying tales of the things they may do to a young boy and girl.'

'We must try,' said Rhiannon resolutely, 'but we need to be well prepared, it may be a long journey.'

They stood up and went back into the woods to search for food. Brychan scouted around and found a family of hedgehogs asleep under a pile of leaves, then he collected some wood and lit a fire. He wrapped the hedgehogs in clay and began cooking them on the fire. Meanwhile, Rhiannon had found a bird in a snare she and her friends had set the day before. It was a large plump thrush. She carefully plucked as many feathers as she could manage before handing it to Brychan to roast on the fire. While he was attending to the hedgehogs and the bird, she disappeared once more to gather some of the huge mushroom-shaped truffles that grew in profusion around the base of the trees. She went down to the stream and drew some water that she placed in a leather pouch hanging at her waist.

The friends made a silent but enjoyable meal of the meat from the hedgehogs, the thrush and the truffles, and drank the cold clear water.

'Do you have any weapons to protect you?' asked Rhiannon.

'I have my father's dagger and this shield,' said the boy, producing the dagger from the belt at his side. Rhiannon had seen the shield, an oblong piece of wood, strengthened with leather and engraved metal bosses. She watched the dagger's wide blade glinting in the sunlight as Brychan brandished it in the air.

Rhiannon had also armed herself with a dagger she had found in her home. She tugged at the long thick creepers growing along the trees and wound them around her waist and over her shoulder. They would make useful ropes, she thought.

'I'm ready,' she said. And the two friends set off down the hill and into the valley.

Rhiannon and Brychan made their way down the hillside in the direction of Coed-y-Caerau. As they came down into the valley, they could smell wood burning and the scuffling noises of animals, restlessly pawing the ground. They drew nearer, leading Llwyd and Brychan's house, Serenwen, so as to make less noise, and began to make out the wooden palisade of the Roman marching camp. They tied the horses loosely to a small bush and crept forward as close as they dared. They stepped carefully forward, locating the ditch and wriggled quietly forward until they were able to lie on their stomachs, hidden in the midst of some thick long grass.

They looked up carefully, and saw the Roman guards on duty outside one of the main gates. They watched silently as the soldiers paraded up and down, then stopped and stood faces towards the hills, eyes alert for any sign of enemy movements.

'I wonder if my father is in there?' whispered Rhiannon.

'He might be,' replied Brychan.

He was looking at one of the guards, he was dark-skinned with curly, dark hair. Something in his manner made Brychan think he was somehow different from the others. His face looked less brutal, his eyes less hard than the other soldiers.

'How are we going to find my father?' whispered Rhiannon.

Two of the guards began walking towards them. Their hearts began beating faster as they thought they had been discovered! But the soldiers stopped within a half a metre of where they lay hidden and began speaking.

'How is our visitor Aemilius?'. The soldier was speaking in his own language, Latin. These words were unfamiliar to Rhiannon, but Brychan had learned some of this language from his teacher, Cynan.

Brychan listened intently.

'He seems pretty sick, Gaius,' said the one called Aemilius. 'We've tied him up with the animals.'

'Animals together,' said Gaius with a sarcastic grin. 'He should make a good slave with proper training, but I expect Legate Aulus Maximus Ostorius will want to question him about any more Silurian plans to attack. They are the most stubborn barbarian force I have faced. They should have been exterminated years ago!

Gaius and Aemilius moved away from the two listeners and returned to their posts near the gates.

Brychan and Rhiannon continued to look and listen, almost afraid to breathe in case they were discovered.

'We have done quite well.' The voice was that of Gaius. 'He seems to be one of the leaders judging by the gold torc he wore round his neck. These Silurians like their jewellery! Anyway, I have taken that piece of gold away from him, I can sell it in the local market.'

'It is supposed to have some magic power,' said Aemilius uneasily. 'I'd be careful if I were you.'

'Rubbish,' said Gaius, 'you are too superstitious! Besides, our mighty god, Mithras will protect me from any of their puny gods.'

'That may be so, but still we were lucky to catch him. The Silurians fight well and bravely. Thank goodness we have spies like . . .'

Brychan cursed as their voices faded away. They had moved away from the fire and were standing further off.

Then their voices became clearer once more as they strolled nearer to the wooden fence.

'. . . He told us about the Silurian ambush and we were able to turn the tables on them.'

How Brychan wished he could have heard the name of this traitor!

'What do you think they will do with Caradog when they have finished their interrogation? asked Aemilius.

'I don't know,' said Gaius. 'they may kill him, or send him into the arena or even send him to Rome for the parade of prisoners. It depends how important they think he is.' He chuckled. 'We could have some fun when we get back to the fort. We could send him into the arena with some wild wolves we've been keeping there. I fancy Caradog will have a tough time trying to save his skin against those animals, we've been starving them for days. Or we could see how he fares against Maelgwyn the gladiator.

We've trained him well since we captured him and he would fight to the death. These Celts are all alike when they have their backs to the wall.

'Perhaps we should think twice about risking Caradog's death,' said Aemilius. 'It's all very well having fun with the prisoners, but the legate may want to keep him in one piece, in case they want to parade him in Rome, show him off to the people, a Silurian leader in chains.'

RHIANNON'S GIFT

The two friends return home and tell Hywel that Caradog has been betrayed and imprisoned. Meirion speaks of Rhiannon's special gifts. Hywel asks her to go back to the Roman camp.

BRYCHAN shuddered as he thought of the fate being planned for Caradog. He knew a little about the barbarous games the Romans played, throwing people in with wild animals or making them fight each other to the death. He thought of Caradog, determined not to betray his people however much the Romans might hurt him! And who was the Silurian spy? He wished he could have heard the name before the soldiers moved away. A spy in their camp! He must try to find out who it was!

Brychan could not stop himself from thinking about wolves with open slobbering jaws and giant gladiators wielding wicked looking swords against a defenceless, naked Silurian warrior.

'Tell me what they are saying,' she whispered.

Brychan glanced across at his friend, 'I don't think you want to know,' he said hoarsely.

'Don't be silly,' her voice was brusque. 'I know how the Romans treat their prisoners. I just want to know where my father is, so that Hywel can rescue him.'

Brychan was silent. He did not know about the images in her mirror or about Llwyd. All he knew was that Rhiannon was a brave girl, and loved her father very much. He did not think she would want to know what the Romans had planned for her father.

Brychan told her what he had overheard from the Roman soldiers. Rhiannon shuddered as he mentioned the wolves and the gladiator, but she put on a brave face and said, 'It won't come to that, he will be rescued before they can do any of those wicked things.'

Brychan said nothing. 'I think we should be getting back before our luck runs out. We are lucky we have not been discovered already.'

The two friends began to ease their way out of the ditch. They scrambled through the bracken and made their way back to the place where they had left Llwyd and Serenwen. Soon they were on their way home–to Pengelli and Hywel.

Hywel looked at Rhiannon, she was standing in front of him, flushed and defiant. Brychan stood solemnly by her side. A number of the people of Pengelli had gathered when they heard of Rhiannon's return. Branwen's brother, Emyr and Rhidian were there, with Arianwen, grieving for her beloved Rhodri, but angry and ready to do battle against the hated enemy who had murdered her husband.

Brychan noticed Bledri slipping in and standing at the back of the crowd, 'He doesn't want people to notice him,' thought Brychan, 'but why? And where has he been to appear so flushed. Has he been running or has he returned from a vigorous ride?' Brychan was always suspicious of Bledri's movements, he knew from experience that the boy was usually up to no good.

'What made you think of such a harebrained scheme?' Hywel said crossly. 'You might have been caught and imprisoned with your father. You might have put him in even greater danger.' Hywel's anger was mingled with relief at his niece's safe return. He was grief-stricken over Rhodri's death and Caradog's capture and felt the sudden responsibilities of leadership keenly. Hywel was a brave and fierce warrior, but he did not relish the burden of leadership, he had always been content to follow his brother. He would have given his life for Caradog and he felt the same deep feeling for Rhiannon. He was upset because she had put herself in so much danger and thankful that she had come to no harm.

'Her father's daughter,' he thought with some exasperation.

'Perhaps she is guided by a stronger force which is beyond your comprehension.' All eyes turned to Meirion, the Druid who was standing nearby, listening to Hywel's tirade.

'The Rhiannon after whom your niece was named also possessed wisdom beyond her years. People listened to her and followed her advice. Who is to say that our own Rhiannon is not also blessed with the courage and wisdom of a woman twice her age. I think we would be wise if we listened to her and took heed of her words.'

Rhiannon thought about the mirror and wondered if Meirion knew of its strange powers.

'I don't feel very wise,' she said, but I do know that I will do my utmost to help in my father's rescue.'

'Tell us what you found out?' Hywel said to Rhiannon in a quieter tone. He held Meirion in the greatest esteem, and always respected his advice.

'We managed to get near to the Roman marching camp and were able to eavesdrop on some of the soldiers talking. They spoke in their own tongue, but Brychan was able to understand most of what they said. Tell my uncle what you overheard,' she said to her friend.

'They talked about throwing Caradog to the wolves or making him fight the gladiator Maelgwyn,' said Brychan. 'Then they said that he would probably be shipped out to Rome to be paraded in chains before the people.'

'I know Maelgwyn,' said Emyr, 'he was the best of our fighters, then he was captured and imprisoned for a long time. I heard that they have been training him as one of their gladiators. Now he is forced to fight for his life in their sick games.'

'I also heard them talk about a spy, someone from our own camp who informed on our ambush.' Brychan paused. 'I didn't hear the name. Anyway, they seemed to be determined to take Caradog to Rome.'

'In chains, humiliated like his namesake,' said Emyr, cryptically.

'Not if we can help it,' said Hywel.

Hywel looked at the two friends as they stared back at him, Rhiannon's eyes were moist, Brychan looked troubled.

'You have done well,' he said, a little more softly. 'We now know for certain that Caradog was captured and taken to the fort at Brynpwca.

Emyr and I are grateful for your information, and we will act on it. But I wish we knew more about the spy, he may be among us at this moment, listening to us and getting ready to take information back to the enemy. If we knew who he was and exactly what the Romans planned for Caradog, we would be stronger and better prepared.'

Rhiannon looked at her uncle, her face resolute. 'Let us go once more to seek information.' We know our way, and we have shown that we are capable of looking after ourselves. Besides, we are not yet warrior-trained, and you need all your best trained warriors when you set out to rescue my father.'

'No,' said Hywel, 'I cannot knowingly risk your life, Caradog would expect me to protect you.'

'You should think of Meirion's advice.' Hywel turned surprised to hear Branwen's voice. Rhiannon's mother continued, 'I have lost my husband, and I do not know if he will ever return.

I do not want to lose my daughter as well. But I believe that Meirion is right. She is a very special child. I have always known it. After listening to her now, I am sure of it. Let her go.'

'And you know, there is also Llwyd,' said Rhiannon.

'We all know how highly you think of Llwyd,' said Hywel, 'and perhaps you are not far wrong. Anyway, I think I am outnumbered. I will let you go, on condition that you promise not to recklessly put yourself into danger. You must promise to hide, listen and return, do not try to do anything foolhardy.'

'I promise,' she said.

She thought again of the pictures in the mirror, and began to feel that the way she was taking was her way, Rhiannon's way, a way that had been destined for her.

RHIANNON IN DANGER

Rhiannon decides to follow her destiny.

RHIANNON lay in the rough comforting straw of her own bed, slumbering fitfully under the warm blankets. She dreamed of the last few days, of her venture to the Roman marching camp, of her father enduring she knew not what. How she wished things were as they had been before the Romans came! She would have given anything to be a little girl again, playing in the fields with her sister Gweneira. Or laughing with joy as she rode down to the Great Water with Brychan and Eirlys, Morwen and Euros. Oh! what fun they had, what happy times! They spent endless days looking for blackberries, wild strawberries or violets (especially the rare white ones). Sometimes they ran through the fields for no reason at all, except the joy of running and feeling the warm breeze on their faces. They often lay in the grass chewing the long green stalks, looking up at the blue sky, thinking that life was an endless succession of long summer days and cool nights.

Her dream changed. She was looking into the mirror her father had given to her, and saw him, fit and handsome, telling her how he would drive the Romans from their land. Then, the image changed to a heap of rags dumped on a mud floor. Shadowy figures moved near by, figures in Roman dress. One of the figures kicked the heap of rags and horrified, she saw her father trying to avoid the blow, groaning with pain. His face was gaunt and haggard.

Suddenly, she sat up in bed, wide-awake. Her father was not there. He was in the hands of the enemy. Oh, what could she do? She thought of Meirion's words:

'Who is to say that our own Rhiannon is not also blessed with the courage and wisdom of a woman twice her age.'

Well she did not feel wise or brave, but she knew that she would do what was expected of her, and venture out once more and find out exactly where her father was and what the Romans were doing to him.

Cocks crowed, pigs squealed, people chattered, as Rhiannon stirred. Light was streaming into the hut. As she opened her eyes, she saw her mother beginning her daily tasks. She flung the blanket from her and rolled out of bed. Things did not seem so bleak in the daytime.

'Good morning, Mother, that bread smells good.'

Branwen was bringing the loaves from the oven.

'You'll need a good breakfast this morning to put some packing into you after your adventure yesterday.'

Rhiannon's mother believed that a good meal was the answer to every problem.

Branwen was a sensible practical woman, who did not easily show her feelings. But this morning, although she affected to be the same as she always was, her voice held a slight tremor. She would not show her feelings to her daughter, that was not her way, but she loved her all the same, and had worried when she had gone missing. She knew also that her husband may never return to her alive. She was a high-principled woman who controlled her feelings well, but now, the prospect of her husband's fate filled her with dread. She had listened to Meirion and Hywel at the meeting, and she feared that her daughter's mission also was quite likely to put her in great danger.

'Come and eat your breakfast. I've prepared a bag of food for you for your journey.'

Rhiannon quickly dressed and ate the bread her mother had baked. As she turned to leave, her mother gave her a quick hug. Then Rhiannon stepped through the door of the hut and made her way to the stables.

'Good morning Rhidian,' she called.

Rhidian was grooming her horse Llwyd. He did not look up. You've a fine morning ahead of you,' he said. 'Llwyd is in fine fettle today.'

Rhidian was stockily built, Rhiannon watched his strong forearms and large capable hands as he brushed the gleaming hindquarters of Llwyd. The horse stamped the ground with his hooves impatiently. He was ready to bear his mistress wherever she wished to go.

Rhidian stood up. 'There,' he said, 'now your Llwyd is ready for anything!'

Rhiannon took hold of the bridle and swung herself up onto the horse's back. She felt the hard warmth of his body beneath her as she turned his head in the direction of the wood.

She saluted Rhidian who raised his hand in farewell.

As Llwyd clip-clopped along the track through the dark woods, Rhiannon listened to the lazy buzzing of insects and the chirruping birdsong.

She was alert to any danger of a marauding Roman, but she saw only a lone hedgehog snuffling in the grass, reminding her of the meal she had shared with Brychan. What a long time ago that seemed! Yet only two days had passed.

Llwyd, sure-footed on familiar paths, made his way through the tall trees, their leaves reaching upward in search of the sun. As she made her way along the path, she left the usual signs for Brychan and her uncles. A carefully broken twig here, a mark in the undergrowth, a strand of cloth or hair, these were secret signs known only to her friends.

Girl and pony reached the edge of the wood and came out into the sunlight. She turned her gaze to the right and Coed-y-Caerau, where she and Brychan had overheard the Roman plans to take Caradog to the fort at Brynpwca. The girl turned Llwyd downhill in the direction of the sea. They reached the main road and Rhiannon turned Llwyd's head in the direction of Brynpwca.

THE ROMAN CAMP

The soldiers carry out their daily routine. Caradog endures the brutality of his imprisonment. Rhiannon overhears Bledri's treachery, and is captured by Esca.

'. . . ite, . . . ite, . . . ite.' The Romans were doing their customary exercise drill.

The soldiers were marching round the parade ground. They were carrying full packs.

'You're getting soft,' snarled optio Suetonius Claudius Tullus. He was second in command to centurion, Marcus Quintus Lutorius and was particularly zealous in drilling the soldiers; he was working hard for promotion.

'You've only been marching for two hours and you're sweating like pigs. Call yourselves Roman, I can see your heads hanging from a Silurian belt if you can't do better than this!'

Hilarion, sweating under the load, muttered something under his breath.

'Barley rations for you, Hilarion, and two days extra drill.'

Hilarion had not realised that Suetonius had such keen hearing.

'He has to stop soon,' whispered Varrius to Hilarion, 'even he must be getting hungry!

'And a flogging for you Varrius, discipline is the watchword for a Roman soldier. We can't let you out amongst these Silures until you are fully fit, otherwise you will not last long.'

No-one else grumbled. All they wanted was to take off their heavy load and rest their aching limbs.

The drilling continued.

Two soldiers were throwing heavy javelins at a large wooden stake in the middle of the parade ground. They carried heavy wicker shields that seemed to weigh a ton. Another two were practising with short heavy swords, stabbing at another wooden stake. Centurion Marcus was urging them on.

'Go for the belly. Thrust. Go in under his guard. Keep yourself covered with your shield when you withdraw.'

The camp was laid out in a square, with the commander's headquarters situated at the centre of the camp; the inside of the square was divided into rows and the tents were pitched along these rows. They were pitched some distance from the perimeter so that they could not easily be fired on with any enemy missiles. A trench had been dug around the outside of the camp and the soil had been made into a mound with a wooden palisade erected on it.

After the exercises and drill, the camp bustled with activity. The soldiers began cooking their breakfast. Some of the auxiliaries tended the horses and other animals, or polished up the armour and military equipment to make sure they were immaculate and ready for battle.

Caradog felt his aching shoulder. The thrust of the sword had plunged in just above the armpit. The blood was encrusted, the flesh black and blue. He ran his hand from his neck up over the top of his head. He had felt a sharp blow on the back of his skull before he lost consciousness. This was the first time he had been awake to take stock of his surroundings. He heard the stamp of horses' hooves and their snorting noises as they waited impatiently for food and grooming. The animals were impatient with being tied up, they were eager for exercise, for a gallop across field, open moor land, forest, and sea beaches. Caradog shared their impatience. He too was hungry. He looked around him.

They had tied him against a post that he shared with a mule. The thongs of leather cut into his wrists and ankles. He heard the sound of footsteps and saw a young soldier coming towards the horses and mules. Although he was dressed in Roman fashion, Caradog recognised him as a Celtic auxiliary.

'Who are you?' Caradog addressed him in his native tongue.

The youth's head twitched. He obviously understood.

'Esca,' he muttered. 'I don't want anything to do with you, I'm a Roman soldier, I won't be doing anything to help you or your tribe, so understand that from the beginning. I am as much your enemy as the soldiers from Rome.'

'Worse,' responded Caradog. 'They are true to their country and birth, but you are a traitor.'

'AAAAAH!' Caradog cried out with pain as Esca kicked him viciously in the side.

'Now do you understand!' said Esca. 'Keep quiet, or you will get more of my boot. Leave me in peace to look after the other animals.' He grinned at his sarcasm.

Caradog watched as Esca fed and watered the horses and mules before moving off in the direction of the cooking pots and campfires.

'No food or drink for me then,' thought Caradog. This did not surprise him. He knew that starvation was part of their strategy to weaken the prisoners before interrogation. He shifted his body to try to get into a more comfortable position.

He thought of his daughter Rhiannon. He knew that Hywel would be leading his people to the rescue. He did not know what they planned, but

Rhiannon's Way

he knew that he could count on them. He only had to be patient and wait.

Meanwhile, Rhiannon had reached the fort and dismounted quietly. She too heard the noises of the awakening camp. She tapped Llwyd on the hindquarters. He moved away from her to give her room to reconnoitre, but he had her in his sights as he quietly cropped the grass.

The girl got down on her stomach and crawled forward through the long grass. She could feel its coolness and smell its comforting bitter smell as she inched forward as far as she dared, to look and listen.

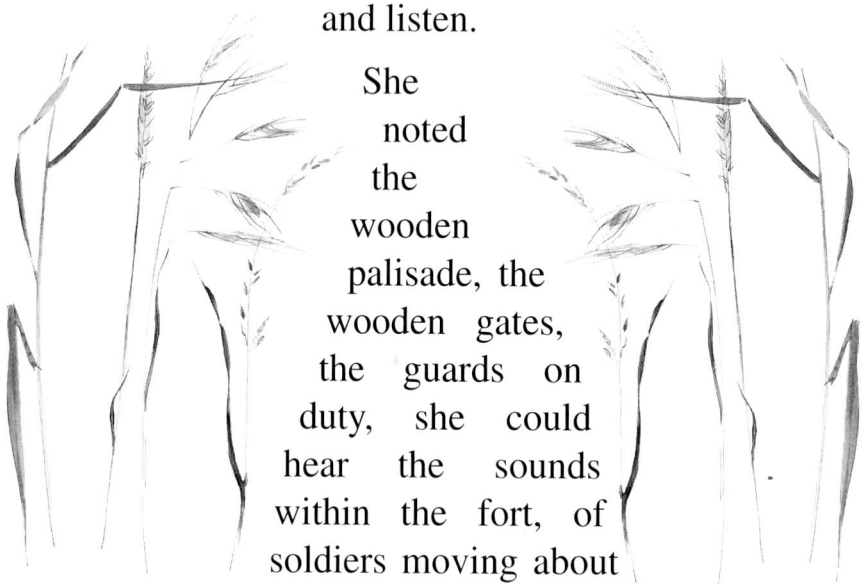

She noted the wooden palisade, the wooden gates, the guards on duty, she could hear the sounds within the fort, of soldiers moving about their daily task, she listened to the murmur of voices and could smell the burning wood of the camp fires. For some reason, she thought of the image she had seen in her mirror, of a sick man in rags lying slumped on a mud floor tied against the back of a beast. She gave a stifled sob as she thought of her father in the hands of a merciless enemy.

She crawled round to a different vantage point and noted another entrance. This, too, was well guarded; again, she shifted her position, and managed to reach the back of the fort.

'I wonder where they will take him, she thought. She shuddered as she recalled Brychan's words, 'They had talked of throwing him to the wolves or making him fight Maelgwyn the gladiator.'

She was close to the guards again and wriggled a little nearer to try to hear what they had to say. She did not think it would help, they would be speaking Latin and she was not familiar with that language.

'Are they going to set him against Maelgwyn or the wolves?'

To her surprise, Rhiannon understood what they were saying. Then she realised that they were speaking in the Celtic tongue. They must be some of the auxiliaries, traitors! She could not see the speakers but she thought that one of them had a familiar voice, which she could not quite place.

Bledri was talking to Esca. 'I don't know,' said Esca, 'he is a great Silurian leader, a prize for the Romans. They may want to take him back in one piece to parade him in Rome. After that they might kill him or sell him for a slave.'

'Pity,' said Bledri, 'I could enjoy seeing him fight Maelgwyn. Caradog wouldn't stand much chance in his present shape.' He sighed, 'You're probably right, in which case, they'll be preparing him for the journey soon no doubt.' The two villains stood up, and began to move away from the tent.

'I must get back,' said Bledri, 'or they will suspect something. I can ride through the night and slip back into Pengelli without anyone being the wiser.'

Esca said nothing. He did not particularly like Bledri, but then not many people did. But he was useful to the Romans at the moment and Esca did not want to cross him unnecessarily. Bledri melted away into the shadows.

Rhiannon waited until the voices ceased and listened as the footsteps moved further away, when she judged it safe to wriggle around, still lying on the grass out of sight. She crawled on her elbows and knees towards Llwyd and did not see the shadowy figure behind her until it was too late. She felt a thudding blow on the base of her neck before she lost consciousness.

Esca dragged Rhiannon back to the other guards.

'A Silurian girl,' said Hilarion. 'We'd better take her inside and show her to the legate. He can decide what to do with her.'

Llwyd stayed perfectly still. He lifted his head and looked steadfastly at Esca as he dragged Rhiannon through the gates of the camp. His ears were laid back flat. He looked back in the direction of Pengelli.

Rhiannon's Way

With one last look back at the Roman fort, he gave a snort and a whinny, and set off at a gallop home.

FRIENDS AND ENEMIES

Brychan goes in search of Rhiannon, he discovers Llwyd and returns to Pengelli. Hywel calls a Council of War. Brychan tells Hywel of his suspicions regarding Bledri.

BRYCHAN'S brain was overactive, he could not sleep. He tossed and turned, thinking of the events of the last few days. He was always exhilarated by Rhiannon's company, she was so full of energy and confidence. But she was sometimes too headstrong and he often feared for her safety. He knew how much she thought of her father and was afraid that her concern for him now that he was in the hands of the Romans would lead her into danger. Meirion had said that he believed that she, like the great Rhiannon of the story, was fulfilling some kind of destiny. Hywel respected the wise priest's words and had decided that Rhiannon could be trusted to find out more of Caradog's fate. Brychan knew that he would do everything in his power to protect her and keep her from harm.

At last he fell into a deep slumber and when the cock crowed it failed to wake him. Sunshine streaming onto his face forced him to open his eyes. His first thoughts were of Rhiannon.

He forgot for a moment the events of yesterday and thought of the last day they had gone riding together. He remembered the day well. It had been the day before he and Rhiannon had gone down to the Roman marching camp. He thought about the way his own horse, Serenwen, failed to keep up with Llwyd. But then, Llwyd was usually faster, especially so when they rode to Cefnllwyd. When they turned the horses' heads in the direction of the holy place, Llwyd had pricked up his ears, eyes alert, and flew like the wind to the top of the open moorland. The ponies had reached the top of the ridge and the two friends looked down on the Great Water and the lush green valley.

Rhiannon loved riding. Brychan had watched her as a gentle breeze stirred her hair. She had sat motionless on her pony's back. In this silent place, there were no animals, no people, only one beautiful majestic buzzard that circled, sweeping along the hidden breeze, riding the air, before hovering and dropping like a stone into the hidden moorland.

The standing stones were the only sign of the human past on this silent, lonely landscape of tough mountain grass and furze. The stones lay scattered just below the summit of the hill. Brychan had seen the shape of the ancient cairn, some of its stones fallen away at some distance from the burial place. He had wondered what great poets or warriors were remembered there. The children never went near the holiest places, the great circle of stones, where the druids performed the sacred ceremonies.

At such times, he was glad he was learning to memorise the great stories of the past. He hoped one day to be like Cynan, the great bard and teacher.

'You have to have a feel for it,' Cynan would say. 'Not everyone is chosen. But you Brychan, will be the best of our bards.'

Brychan flushed with pleasure when Cynan talked like this, he had worked hard at the lessons, and could remember many of the great stories but he had a long way to go. Most of Brychan's friends were in Cynan's class. The class also included Bledri.

Bledri was the only child of Ceiriog who was a warrior prince and highly respected by the people of Pengelli. He was also a wealthy farmer. His son was small and dark and vain and used his father's position to further his own ends. Bledri was quick at his lessons, but, unfortunately for him, Brychan was always a little bit better at everything. So, Bledri hated him, but he cloaked his dislike beneath his smile. In fact he was a boy who smiled a lot, but in spite of his smiles, the other boys did not really trust him. He wanted to be one of the circle of friends and he went along with their plans, and did them favours when they asked. And he bought things for them, because his father was rich. Yet in spite of all his efforts to curry favour, the other boys shunned him as much as they dared, and he spent much of his time on his own.

He had a particular dislike for Brychan because Brychan was not only cleverer than he was, Brychan could also make people laugh. People laughed with Brychan, but they laughed at Bledri, and Brychan sometimes joined in the laughter. Bledri could not forgive him for that. To make matters worse, Brychan was becoming one of Cynan's favourite pupils He even expected him to win the highest award–the Gold Branch! Not if Bledri could help it! He would do anything to bring shame on Brychan even lying, stealing, and cheating. How he hated him! But Bledri kept these feelings to himself for the time being and kept on smiling and biding his time. Brychan knew that Bledri did not like him, but he did not know the extent of Bledri's hatred. Brychan was generally kind and trusting, the sort of boy who could not attribute evil thoughts to anyone. This made him popular, but vulnerable.

Brychan stirred and got out of bed. Thinking now of the previous day's activities, he quickly dressed and walked across to Rhiannon's home. He was looking forward to talking to her and listening to her plans for their next journey.

Branwen was feeding the chickens. 'Where's Rhiannon?' asked Brychan.

'I don't know,' responded Branwen. 'I haven't seen her for some time.'

'She's probably gone to our place in the wood,' he thought, bade Branwen good day and went up to the stables to get his horse, Serenwen.

Swinging himself up onto the horse's back he turned its head in the direction of the wood. Quietly he made his way to their hiding place. No, there was no sign of Rhiannon. Or was there? His heart missed a beat. He noticed a strand of wool on a branch of the tree. He recognised it came from Rhiannon's cloak. Then she had been there earlier. But where was she?

He began to track through the wood and came upon other tell-tale signs. Signs that he knew Rhiannon had left for him. He made his way down through the countryside following her well-laid tracks and signs. His heart was racing. What had possessed her to go down alone? Why hadn't she waited for him? He was afraid something like this would happen.

She was too headstrong. He knew she was practised in all kinds of woodcraft and the Romans would be hard put to be aware of a Silurian girl roaming about in her own territory. But accidents could happen. Brychan's heart stopped as he thought what the Romans might do to her if they caught her. He knew they were merciless.

As Serenwen turned his head in the direction of Coed-y-Caerau, Brychan saw a familiar looking horse and rider galloping towards Brynpwca. He recognised Brith and Bledri! Why was he going at such a pace towards the Roman fort? thought Brychan. Surely Bledri was an unlikely person to risk his life for Caradog? Unless there was a more sinister explanation for his sudden departure! A tiny suspicion came into Brychan's mind. An idea that he would rather dismiss! He thought again of the soldier's conversation.

'. . . we were lucky to catch him. The Silurians fight well and bravely. Thank goodness we have spies like . . . He told us about the Silurian ambush and we were able to turn the tables on them.'

What if the name he had not been able to hear was Bledri? Brychan hoped that he was wrong. He did not like Bledri but if it were true, Ceiriog and Bledri's mother, Llun, would be heartbroken.

As he continued on his way following Rhiannon's signs, Brychan was wrapt in thought, pondering on this new discovery.

Suddenly he heard faint but familiar sounds. A pony's cough! The impatient stamping of a horse's hoof! He looked through the trees and saw Llwyd standing at the edge of the wood, riderless!

Quietly, Brychan made his way to the pony, and moved in as close as he could get. Llwyd did not move. Where was Rhiannon? Llwyd would not have come back without her unless she was in deep trouble! As the boy moved closer still, the horse looked up and gazed at Brychan with its beautiful deep brown eyes. It whinnied distressfully, as Brychan jumped from Serenwen and took hold of Llwyd's mane.

'What's the matter boy,' he said in a soothing voice, 'where's your mistress? Where's Rhiannon?' Llwyd laid his ears flat on his head, snorting, his beautiful eyes rolled around in distress. He turned his head in the direction of the Roman fort at Brynpwca and stamped his hooves impatiently. Brychan shuddered. He hoped that his worst fears had not been realised. But Llwyd would never leave Rhiannon behind unless she had been captured and taken into the fort. Sadly, the boy remounted Serenwen and returned slowly home followed by Llwyd.

Pengelli was bustling with the work of the day. Smoke was rising from Rhidian's smithy as he went about his daily tasks. Cynan was giving a lesson to a few boys. Hywel, Emyr, Arianwen, and Rhodri were preparing their weapons of war.

Rhiannon's Way

Gwyn was in the stables inspecting the horses and chariots. Ceiriog, on his horse, Gwennant, had left the camp and was on his way to his own farmstead to inspect his sheep and cattle.

Brychan signalled for the gate to open and leading Llwyd, he rode through on Serenwen.

Arianwen was the first to rush to their side.

'What's happened? Where have you been?' she cried anxiously. She looked at Llwyd in dismay. 'Where's Rhiannon?'

'I hope I am not right,' said Brychan, 'but I think she went to the Roman fort. I found Llwyd on his way back to Pengelli. He wouldn't leave

Rhiannon unless she had been captured! His face was grim.

'Hywel! Emyr!' Arianwen shouted to the men and they rushed to where Brychan stood by Serenwen's side; Llwyd was pawing the ground. Gwenllian and Collen, their wives, hearing the noise, ran from their houses and all gathered around Brychan.

Pale-faced but composed, Branwen stood at her door as Brychan led Llwyd towards her.

Hywel looked at the people gathered expectantly around Llwyd, Branwen and Brychan. 'We need a full Council,' he said 'Let's go to the Great Hall.'

The Great Hall was full. Hywel stood in the centre, Emyr and Arianwen by his side.

He looked at his people, as they stood or sat expectantly waiting for him to speak.

Rhidian held Cigfa's hand, Arianwen's children, Rhys, Pryderi and Chwerthin sat at their feet.

Emyr's wife, Collen sat with her three daughters, Heulwen, Delwyn and Ehedydd,

Hywel's wife, Gwenllian played with the braids of her long fair hair and her father, Meirion the Druid, stood behind her, composed and grave, a tall imposing figure with his flowing dark cloak, his long grey hair and his bird-like piercing eyes. Her children, Iorwerth, Eleri and Euros played idly with the wools and dyes lying close by.

Brychan stood near his parents, Gwyn and Eirlys, his sister, Morwen held his hand tightly.

Cynan had taken his seat at the back of the hall with his wife, Aurwen, and their children, Arianrhod and Cenwyn.

The hall full of people waited expectantly to hear from their new leader.

Hywel stood near the fire, looking grave and dignified.

'You know why we are here. We have lost Caradog and Rhodri in the fighting. Rhodri died for our cause,' he paused and glanced at Arianwen. She was sitting composed, although when he mentioned her husband's name her mouth tightened and her demeanour became more determined.

Hywel continued, 'Brychan and Rhiannon have given us information which makes us think that Caradog may be held prisoner by the Romans. We think he may be at the fort at Brynpwca. As some of you know, I asked Rhiannon to go out again and bring us more information of Caradog's whereabouts and any plans the Romans may have for him. She bravely agreed and set out this morning. Now Llwyd has returned without Rhiannon. We know what this means. Llwyd would not return without her unless she has been captured by the Romans.'

'I think Hywel is right.' It was Bledri's voice.

Brychan looked up in surprise. He had not noticed Bledri slipping into the back of the hall.

'I saw Rhiannon going down to the Roman fort and followed her myself. I saw a Roman auxiliary knock her unconscious and drag her into the fort. I waited to see if I could do anything, but I was on my own. Then I saw Brychan coming down on Serenwen. I saw him taking Llwyd and leading him back to the fort. I've only just arrived back myself. I'm surprised that Brychan didn't go with her in the first place.

He might have been able to warn her about the auxiliary.'

'Why didn't you do something to help her?' asked Brychan angrily.

'It happened too quickly,' replied Bledri defensively. 'I tried to crawl around and find out what was happening to her, but I couldn't see anything. I thought I should get back as soon as possible to warn Hywel.'

Bledri turned again to Hywel, 'We must do what we can to rescue Caradog and Rhiannon. We all know what might happen to them, at best they may become slaves in Rome, at worst they could be killed by gladiators or wild beasts.'

'We know, we know,' said Hywel hastily, he didn't want Branwen to be more distressed than she was already. But she remained impassive, although her face looked even more drawn and gaunt with grief.

'However, Bledri is right, we must prepare to do battle. We need scouts to watch the Roman movements at Brynpwca. As soon as we get word that they are moving we must ambush them.

Brychan, I want you to go with Rhidian to the outpost. Bring us back word as soon as you see any suspicious movements in the vicinity of the Great Water.'

'Bledri, go to your father and tell him what has happened. He is at your farm. I shall need him in the fighting.'

Brychan felt angry with Bledri. He had done nothing himself to help Rhiannon and had managed to imply that Brychan had failed her by not being with her to protect her. He thought of Bledri's explanation of his own actions near the Roman fort. They did not ring true. He was sure he had seen Bledri go through the gates. His suspicions deepened and he knew that he had to speak to Hywel.

Bledri left the Great Hall on his errand to his father, and Hywel issued further instructions to the company.

'I know you are all more than ready to take part in this battle. Our one aim is to rescue Caradog and Rhiannon from the Roman enemy. Go now to your homes and prepare for the battle. I want every warrior in prime fighting condition and ready to go at a moment's notice.'

The people began to disperse, and Brychan turned to Hywel. 'I need to speak to you in private,' he said.

The two sat down by the fire. Everyone had gone and the hall was empty.

'I think that Bledri may be the spy in the camp,' said Brychan.

'You will have to show some proof for such an accusation,' said Hywel quietly.

He liked and trusted Brychan and knew that he was not the kind of boy to accuse anyone without good reason.

'When I went in search of Rhiannon, I saw Bledri making his way to the Roman fort. I could swear that he entered the fort, and he didn't seem to be trying to hide his movements. And his concern for Rhiannon's safety doesn't ring true.' He hesitated, 'Bledri usually thinks of himself, and besides because she is so close to me, you know that he doesn't like me very much.' Brychan had reddened a little as he spoke of his friendship with Rhiannon. 'It's not much to go on, but it may be worthwhile to be a little more cautious when we discuss our plans in front of him, and perhaps a little more watchful of his movements. It won't hurt if we take a little more care.'

Hywel pondered on Brychan's words. He himself was not too fond of Bledri, but then not many people were. And there was some sense in what Brychan said. They knew that there was a spy, and these were the first suspicions anyone had of anyone at Pengelli.

'I will think about what you have said, Brychan, there will certainly be no harm in taking care with any discussions we have about our fighting plans. Thank you for telling me of your suspicions, I know that you would not cast doubt on anyone, even Bledri without due consideration.'

They parted and returned to their own homes to prepare for war.

Pengelli bustled with preparations for the forthcoming battle.

Rhidian meticulously examined every item of equipment, the harness for the horses, the chariots, the chariot wheels and fierce sharp blades. He repaired everything that was necessary and polished the leather and metal until it shone. He knew that his family and friends depended on his skill with their lives. A loose chariot wheel could kill, and soldiers needed sharp swords. The Silurians were skilful horse riders, and Rhidian made sure that the horses were healthy and fit, ready to carry their owners into the thick of battle.

Hywel and Emyr, rode one of the chariots, Arianwen had sometimes ridden with Rhodri, now she planned to ride with Brychan's father, Gwyn. Many of the other warriors of Pengelli were on horseback or on foot. Many of the women would accompany the men, while the smallest children remained in the camp, looked after by the grandparents.

The older folk and young children helped to prepare the dyes and clothes for battle. They mixed the blue woad with which the warriors covered their bodies, and melted and thickened animal fat to form the grease with which they plastered their hair. This grease and paint made the bodies of the warriors slippery, enabling them to move easily, ride quickly and strike terror into the enemy.

The warriors prepared themselves for battle. They examined their swords and shields regularly to ensure that they were in perfect condition. They exercised every day and practised riding, swordplay, and chariot riding. Of all the Celtic tribes, the Silurian warriors were the most feared by their enemies.

Bledri was as busy in the battle preparations as any of the other soldiers. In fact he was seen everywhere. He made sure that his own armour was shining and polished to perfection. He offered to help his father to get ready his chariot. He talked with Rhidian, offering to help with the polishing and cleaning of leather and metal, and grooming the horses. Whenever he engaged people in conversation, he turned the discussion to the battle plans. He hoped that most people would be ready to discuss matters freely with the son of a distinguished warrior like Ceiriog. But

Hywel, alerted to Brychan's suspicions about Bledri, had not yet divulged any important information to anyone. He was biding his time.

When he judged the time to be ripe, Hywel recalled his warriors. They assembled in the Great Hall to hear his words.

'I believe that they will try to ship Caradog across the sea to Rome. There they will undoubtedly parade him in chains to the Roman people and offer him as a slave to the highest bidder. I expect many of the Roman matrons will be attracted to the idea of owning such a handsome Silurian leader. We must do all in our power to prevent this from happening. When we receive word from Brychan and Rhidian, we will set up an ambush. You all know the part of the wood on the slopes leading to the river between Brynpwca and Isca. We will hide in the woods there. The Romans will have to take that road to get to Isca so it is a perfect place to surprise the enemy and with courage and determination we will defeat them and rescue Caradog and Rhiannon.'

Bledri was standing at the back of the crowd of listeners, listening attentively to all that was being said. He slipped quietly away before Hywel had finished speaking.

He swung himself up onto his pony, Brith, having bound cloth around the horse's hooves to muffle the sound as he rode out of the camp.

Treachery In The Enemy Camp

Bledri the betrayer. Bledri rides down to the Roman encampment and talks with Ostorius and Marcus. He tells them of Hywel's plans to ambush the Romans and rescue Caradog.

BLEDRI rode away from Pengelli down the hillside towards Brynpwca. He halted on the outskirts of the Roman fort, dismounted and tied Brith to a twisted old hazel tree. This was the appointed meeting place for the traitor and his Roman friends.

He looked round him cautiously. Esca separated from the other guards and walked slowly towards him, the other soldiers remained close enough to come to his aid in case of trouble.

Esca waited. Bledri swaggered towards him. 'Take me to your centurion,' he commanded, 'I have important news and Brith has had a hard ride.' He turned to his horse, and untied him. Esca pulled the gates open to allow Bledri inside the compound, then he quickly closed them again behind the boy and his horse. Dawn was breaking and soldiers were beginning to move about their accustomed duties in the half-light.

'You'd better see one of the centurions,' muttered Esca. He led Bledri to one of the tents and called out, 'Marcus, sir, someone wants to see you with important news of the Silures.'

'Sir,' called the traitor, 'this is Bledri, I come from Pengelli, I have news of the Silurian battle plans.'

His voice was loud and confident. It carried quite a long way, further than he realised, for it made a certain prisoner's head jerk to attention. Dark blue eyes looked across at the figure in front of the captain's tent and recognised the familiar shape of Ceiriog's son.

'Bledri,' muttered Caradog. 'A traitor!' He sank back into apparent slumber but he was never more alert, straining eyes and ears to take in all he could from his place of imprisonment.

Treachery in the Enemy Camp

Marcus pulled up the flap of his tent. He surveyed Bledri suspiciously, 'It had better be good,' he growled.

Bledri smiled winningly, and bowed, 'I think you will be interested in what I have to say. I have detailed knowledge of the Silurian plans to try to rescue Caradog.' Marcus looked at him in surprise.

'You'd better come in and tell me all you know, I think that Legate Ostorius will want to hear what you have to say.'

Marcus led Bledri into the legate's tent, out of earshot of the listening Caradog, where he recounted Hywel's strategy with all the details of the place where the Silurians planned to lie hidden.

Ostorius sat at the table in the tent listening while Marcus questioned the spy.

'I think I know the place,' said Marcus. 'It is well

thought out. We would be taking that road, if we wanted to ship Caradog to Rome.'

Ostorius sat deep in thought. 'So they are attempting another ambush,' he said. 'The last one didn't work very well, thanks to you, Bledri.' The boy tried unsuccessfully to look modest. 'Thank you boy, your loyalty to the Empire will not go unrewarded.'

Bledri did not like being called 'boy,' but he hoped that the legate or the centurion would take him further into his confidence by telling him of the fate he had in store for Caradog. He was disappointed. Ostorius and Marcus were too shrewd to trust a Silurian spy with their own schemes.

Marcus continued. 'We want to know more of the Silurian warriors and their weapons. We want names and numbers. We also want you to tell us how many people live at Pengelli and how well it is fortified. When we have dealt with this little battle and with Caradog and Rhiannon, we shall want to attack Pengelli itself and your information will be of the greatest assistance.'

Treachery in the Enemy Camp

Bledri began to give the details he was asked for and Marcus called in a scribe to take down the information as Bledri recounted it. He was ready with every detail he had been asked for including the position of the guards' outpost and many of the places where the Silurian warriors were likely to hide before pouncing on the enemy.

When he had finished, Marcus thanked him once more and Bledri gave the Roman salute. Ostorius responded with a tired wave of his hand.

Bledri stood uncertainly, not sure whether he had been dismissed.

'I am glad to be of service,' he said. 'I shall be glad to continue to help you, but I would beg one favour in return.'

Ostorius looked impatient.

'They are all alike,' he thought. 'After their own ends.'

'Well what is it? He asked testily.

'When you engage with the Silurians, there is a boy,' Bledri looked sly. 'I will point him out to you. I would like to be sure that he dies in the fighting.'

81

'I expect all of them to be wiped out, but if it makes you happy, point him out and I will make sure that he does not survive.'

Bledri smiled, bowed, saluted again and left the tent.

Esca was waiting for him outside.

'How could you betray your people like that?' he said angrily.

'You're a fine one to accuse me of betrayal,' said Bledri, 'you are a Celt and you fight for the Romans.'

'I know,' said Esca, 'and there is not a day passes but I feel ashamed. Nevertheless, everyone knows where I stand, while you hide behind smiles and treachery and put your people in danger, without giving them a chance to defend themselves. Your way is the coward's way.'

Bledri was red with anger. 'The Romans are a great people,' he said, 'they are bound to win and conquer the British kingdom. I will use every means at my disposal to help them win that fight. I will get richly rewarded and I will become a Roman citizen, with all the power I could wish for.' He looked scathingly at Esca. 'You will probably die in battle.'

'At least I will die a soldier,' said Esca. He turned on his heel and made his way back to his own quarters, he was too choked with anger and disgust to continue the argument with Bledri.

Caradog lay in pain, thinking about Bledri and his treachery. He felt desperate. 'What hope do we have of defeating the Romans when our own kind are ready to betray us?

Suddenly he heard movement and loud talking. He managed to look around to where the voices came from, and saw Esca and another auxiliary dragging a young girl towards him. She looked familiar.

'Oh the good gods!' Caradog cried, 'not Rhiannon!'

Esca and Bradach (an auxiliary from Brittany) threw Rhiannon down beside her father. Her hands and feet were tied. She was semi-conscious.

'Give her some water, for the sake of your own soul!' begged Caradog. Esca looked at him and then at the girl. His face softened and left them. In a few minutes he returned with a pitcher of water. He threw some over her face and she stirred and moaned. Without saying a word, Esca turned on his heel and left, but he left the pitcher beside the two prisoners.

'You'll get into trouble,' said Bradach.

'Not if you keep quiet,' muttered Esca. 'There's a limit to how much I can take from the Romans. She is only a young girl.'

Caradog shifted across to his daughter. 'How did you get here? How did you get caught?'

She was tearful, but glad to be with her father at last. They embraced as far as they were able.

'What can we do?' muttered Caradog. He felt impotent and angry. He was sick and feverish with his lack of food and with his wounds. Rhiannon tried to comfort him. 'Hywel is gathering our warriors to fight the Romans and rescue us,' she said. 'Don't worry father, all is not lost. I know I shouldn't have allowed myself to be caught but it means that we are together, and we may be able to help each other. Do you think that you can untie the ropes around my wrists?'

Caradog's eyes moistened. His young daughter's courage made him feel ashamed at his own sense of defeat.

He shuffled towards her and they managed to get back to back.

He moved down until he was able to grasp the ropes binding her wrists. After much effort, they began to slacken. After a little while, Rhiannon's hands were free. She was able to give her father something to drink from the pitcher left by Esca. She took some of the cold water herself and felt better. Caradog slumped back, he seemd to slip once more into semi-consciousness.

She heard footsteps and saw Esca returning. He began tending the mules, cleaning out the straw and putting down their food.

'Thank you for the water,' she said as she watched him performing his tasks.

'I'm not supposed to give anything to the prisoners,' he muttered.

'But you gave to us,' she said gently.

'You are a young girl and the man is very ill. Besides you are Celts.'

'So are you I think,' she said.

'From Gaul,' he mumbled.

'So why are you fighting against your own people?'

'It's a long story,' he said. 'My family were all killed and I had to choose between death, slavery or joining the auxiliary force to fight with the Romans. I was young and fit and had fighting experience. Everyone seemed to be joining up. They offered good money. I survive.' His face was solemn.

He looked across at her. 'What's your name?' he asked.

'Rhiannon,' she said.

'I heard a story once,' he said, 'about another Rhiannon.'

'She was dressed in gold and rode a white horse,' said the girl.

Treachery in the Enemy Camp

'In my story, she is lying on a slab of stone, she is surrounded by old hags jeering and spitting on her,' replied Esca.

'I know that story too,' said Rhiannon, 'but she is rescued in the end.' She paused 'So could I be, if you helped us.'

Esca looked at her. She looked very young, but there was something about her. She was lying tied to a pole against her father's slumped body. Her clothes were torn and her hair dishevelled, but her face was animated and there was something about the compelling gaze of her eyes. Esca thought of what might happen to her and he shuddered.

'What can I do?' he asked, his voice sounded despondent.

'If I know that you are our friend,' said Rhiannon, 'I shall know that I can rely on you when the time comes. That may be sooner than you think.'

Esca said nothing, but again turned on his heels and left the two prisoners.

Caradog In Danger

Ostorius calls a meeting to consider ways of disposing of Caradog. The prisoners receive an unexpected offer of help.

LEGATE Ostorius called the Tribune Cassius Ligarius Lepidus and two of the senior centurions into the Praetorium tent, one of the centurions was Marcus Quintus Lutorius.

'We need to discuss the matter of Caradog,' said Ostorius. 'He is becoming more feeble by the hour, we may have to crucify him or strangle him out of the way.'

'There is also the girl,' said Marcus.

'Yes, well, let's decide what to do with Caradog first,' said Ostorius 'What do you think Lepidus?'

The tribune replied with feeling. 'The Silurians have been a stubborn race and they need to be taught a sharp lesson. I agree with Ostorius,

Caradog is very feeble, he would not survive the long journey to Rome and would be so much unnecessary expense. Killing him here would show the barbarians that we mean business.'

Marcus nodded, 'Thanks to their traitor Bledri, we know where they will be lying in wait for us if we take the road to Isca. I suggest that we let the wolves have a go at him, that way we will provide good entertainment for the soldiers and humiliate the Silurian people.'

'What do we do with the girl?' mused Ostorius.

'She will make a useful slave in Rome,' said Marcus.

Having agreed on the fate of Caradog and Rhiannon, they dispersed and Marcus went back to his own tent to prepare for the daily session of weapons training. This morning he planned to supervise Esca's practice with sword and shield.

Esca was already on the practice ground with Drusillus. They had been practising for an hour with their large wicker shield and a heavy wooden sword before Marcus joined them. He watched them for a while. 'Go for the belly, Esca,

Caradog in Danger

he shouted, 'thrust, go under his guard.' Esca thrust forward with the sword under his friend's shield and into his belly. Drusillus keeled over in mock death.

'That's enough,' said Marcus. 'I need you to get on with some other jobs. Drusillus clean out the toilets, Esca, get down to the compound where we have those wild wolves. Make sure they are securely tied up. Tell me if they are hungry and bad-tempered enough to enjoy a Silurian meal!' He chuckled.

Esca was horrified but he dared not show any emotion. 'Which Silurian, sir?' he asked.

'The one they call Caradog,' said Marcus. 'He's been lying around too long and is becoming a nuisance.'

'I thought we were taking him to Rome,' said Esca innocently.

'Yes, well, we've decided not to take so much trouble with a worthless savage,' said Marcus shortly. 'Don't ask so many questions and get on with the job.'

Esca saluted smartly and left immediately for the animal compound. Four mean-looking, hungry wolves prowled around inside the animal compound, snarling and snapping as Esca drew near. He checked the gate and the fence surrounding the beasts, then made his way to where Rhiannon and her father lay bound.

Rhiannon was dozing as Esca approached. His footsteps made her look up.

'How are you?' he asked.

Surprised at his apparent concern for their welfare, she replied, 'Hungry and stiff.'

'How is your father?' he asked.

She looked at Esca, slightly puzzled, then looked across at Caradog. He was awake and alert, in spite of his prolonged suffering he still looked dignified.

'What do you want?' he asked the boy. 'You have some bad news I fancy.'

Esca looked at the ground, unable to look them in the eye. 'You are not going to Rome,' he said, 'they have been keeping some wolves back there in the compound.'

Caradog looked grey, but he stopped Esca, 'You needn't say any more, I know what they plan to do.' His look warned Esca that he did not want him to continue in Rhiannon's hearing.

His daughter tossed her head impatiently. 'Don't spare me father,' she said, 'I know what Romans do to prisoners. I am not a child any longer, don't treat me like one.'

She turned to Esca. 'Now we'll see what mettle you really have. Are you going to continue fighting with the enemy or are you going to behave like a true Celt?'

Esca hesitated. At last he said, 'I have had enough of Roman ways. They call us barbarians, how barbaric are the things they do to us? I will help you in any way I can.'

'Can you enter and leave the camp as you please?' asked Rhiannon.

'More or less,' he said. 'I would have to give a reason but I should be able to manage that.'

'Do you think you can delay the . . . ' she shuddered, '. . . the plans they have for my father, and get word to Hywel?'

Esca pondered once more. 'I could say that the beasts are not quite ready,' he said.

'We only need a day or two,' said Rhiannon. 'I know that Hywel and his warriors are fighting fit and ready for battle.'

'I'll do it,' said Esca. 'Leave it to me.'

He was about to leave when Rhiannon held up her hand. 'Wait' she said as she unpinned the brooch on her cloak. 'Take this to Hywel as a sign of good faith. Otherwise, he will not trust you.'

Esca took the brooch and left the two prisoners without another word. He made his way immediately to Marcus' tent.

'The beasts are not quite ready sir,' he said. 'I think they need to be starved for a few more days to give the soldiers a really good show.'

'I'll leave it to you Esca,' said Marcus, 'we are not in that much of a hurry, and I don't care if Caradog goes on suffering for another few days.'

Esca saluted and left him.

The boy had lied to Rhiannon when he said that he could leave the fort whenever he liked. Roman soldiers were not allowed to go out into enemy territory alone. He would have to find a way of getting in and out without anyone knowing. He knew how. He strolled casually to the back of the animal compound and found a loose stake in the palisade surrounding the fort. Moving it around until he had loosened it, he managed to pull it up out of the ground and make a hole big enough for him to wriggle through. In a moment he had fled into the undergrowth and began to make his way to Pengelli. He knew that he had little time and ran like the wind. It was tough going through the woods, uphill all the way, but Esca was fit and a Roman soldier was trained to march 20 miles in five hours. He was outside the Pengelli camp in two and a half.

Brychan and Rhidian were at the look-out post. Brychan saw him first. A young Roman boy running and darting between the trees. A Roman soldier, on his own!

'Kill him,' whispered Rhidian,'

'Wait,' said Brychan. 'Perhaps he will be more useful if we question him, and he may be able to tell us what is happening at the Roman fort.'

'He'd better,' threatened Rhidian. He was in no mood to be merciful to a Roman, he was thinking of his dead brother, Rhodri and his widow Arianwen.

Silently, they descended from the lookout post and crept silently through the wood. They stalked Esca as he moved stealthily through the trees. He stopped for a moment looking around him trying to get his bearings. He felt a thud on the back of his neck and fell to the ground, unconscious.

Brychan and Rhidian dragged him to the large gates of the Pengelli camp and shouted to their guards, 'Let us in Cenwyn, we have a prisoner!'

Cenwyn, Rhys and Morwen opened the huge gates and Brychan and Rhidian dragged in their prisoner. They threw him on the ground and he began to stir. He sat up and rubbed the back of his neck. Looking up, he saw three children staring down at him curiously.

'Am I in Pengelli?' he asked anxiously, 'I need to see Hywel at once, there isn't a moment to lose.'

'Wait,' said Brychan, 'we are not likely to trust a Roman auxiliary soldier, a traitor to our race.'

'I was all those things,' said Esca 'but I have come now to help you. Look at this if you don't believe me.' And he unpinned Rhiannon's brooch from his short cloak. He handed it to Brychan who examined it closely. His face changed, a lump came in his throat as he thought of the danger his friend was facing.

He handed it to Rhidian.

'It is Rhiannon's,' said Rhidian. 'See, here are the magic symbols which keep her from harm.' He pointed out the triskele patterns. 'I would recognise it anywhere.'

'Rhiannon gave it to me to show you,' said Esca, 'so that you would know that I come in peace to give you important news. Please take me to Hywel.'

Brychan and Rhidian looked at each other, and without another word they helped Esca on to his feet and escorted him to Hywel's home.

'Hywel,' they called, 'we have a visitor.'

Hywel emerged from the building and saw Esca standing supported on either side by Brychan and Rhidian. He scowled and reached for his sword. Rhidian held his hand.

'Listen to what the boy has to say,' he said gently. 'He has Rhiannon's brooch as a token of his trustworthiness and he comes with important news.'

Brychan showed Hywel the brooch. 'Come inside,' he growled.

'Well?' he said.

Esca looked desperate. 'You have to act quickly,' he said. 'They are not taking Caradog to Isca, they intend throwing him to the wild beasts. I managed to persuade them to delay for a day or two, but it will happen very soon.' He spoke quickly and urgently.

Hywel's face looked grim. 'I thought they would have taken a great leader like Caradog to Rome, I was wrong. I should have known that they would be far more cruel. Why have you decided to return to your own people?'

'I have watched Romans wreck and destroy everything that stands in their way and say it is in the name of their Empire. I have become sick of being a part of Roman ways. I talked with Rhiannon, and she made me realise that I have good reason to be proud of being a Celt.'

'Rhiannon can be very persuasive,' said Hywel. He stood up briskly. 'Enough talking, it is time to act.'

HYWEL'S STRATEGY

Hywel prepares his warriors and they attack the Roman camp.

HYWEL gathered his warriors in the Great Hall. 'Esca has brought news of the Romans' intentions regarding Caradog,' he said. He paused, then said abruptly, 'They will not be taking him to Rome, they intend to feed him to the wolves.'

An angry murmur rippled through the hall.

'We will not let that happen,' said Hywel grimly. 'We will attack the Brynpwca fort without delay. We know that the Romans do not like to fight at night so we will make our preparations during nightfall and begin our attack just before dawn.'

He sat down with his most distinguished warriors. 'I have fought many battles and I have learned that the Roman camps are always made in exactly the same way,' he said. Using his dagger, he drew a rectangle in the dry mud, then divided it into four quarters. 'They will fortify their camp with a ditch and a wooden palisade.

'Cynan and Gwyn, I want you to take some men and women and gather wood, branches and animal fat. While it is still dark, you will build a fire outside the south end of the palisade and be ready to set fire to it when I give the signal. This will create a diversion and put the Romans in a state of panic.

'Ceiriog prepare your best horses and riders and be ready to breach the main gate. The charioteers will follow the horses and the foot warriors will come behind. I shall want some scouts to deal with the guards.'

Bledri had been standing near the back of the hall, listening intently to the Council of War. He was about to slip through the door when he found his path blocked by Brychan.

'I think not Bledri,' he said quietly. 'You will not be telling your friends of our plans this time.'

'I don't know what you mean,' said Bledri, but he looked pale and his voice shook.

Hywel stood up. 'We know that you have betrayed us already,' he said seriously.

'What proof do you have?' Bledri blustered.

'Yes,' said his father Ceiriog, 'what proof do you have that my son would do such a thing.' He stood up, his body quivering with indignation.

'Not much, until now,' Brychan admitted, 'but Esca has come from the Roman fort, and he witnessed Bledri's treachery.'

Ceiriog, fell silent. He had noticed that Bledri did not show much enthusiasm when people talked of the exploits of Caradog, and he knew that Bledri did not like Brychan. But he did not want to believe that his son, Bledri could be guilty of such deep treachery. Ceiriog himself was a true, loyal Silurian who was respected by all at Pengelli.

Hywel spoke again. 'Make sure that Bledri is held prisoner until we decide what to do with him. His fate will have to wait until we have finished the business at Brynpwca.'

Brychan and Rhidian took firm hold of Bledri's arms and marched him out of the Great Hall.

The Silurians gathered on the hillside at dead of night, their multi-coloured dragon standards furled, the warriors silent.

Meirion the Druid asked the spirits for a blessing and prayed in the holy place. He exhorted them to bravery, reminding them of other famous victories, of the famous warrior Caratacus after whom their leader had been named. And of Boudicca who had faced the Romans courageously and died with glory.

In the Roman fort, at Brynpwca, Hilarion awoke, stirred and stumbled out of bed. He began to make his way to the toilets. If he had looked up at the hillside he might have seen a glinting through the trees, if he had noticed, he would have thought it was the first morning light. But Hilarion was preoccupied with his preparations for his stint of guard duty. The warriors moved silently down the hillside and through the woods, Cynan and Gwyn with their people bore the pile of wood and grease quietly to the south end of the palisade. Gwyn dealt with the guards and they began to pile up the branches and spreading the grease over them ready for the blaze.

Hywel's Strategy

Ceiriog waited with his horsemen above the gate, well hidden by the trees. Hywel held the chariot reins tightly, his knuckles showed white but he remained still and composed. They were waiting for first light.

The sky above the horizon began to turn colour, and Hywel gave a whispered command. A lark cried and Cynan looked at Gwyn and nodded. They set fire to the pile of wood. At first the Romans did not notice the smoke, it was near the animal compound and there were never many soldiers near there. Esca and Brychan dispatched the guards at the gates and Ceiriog and his horsemen burst through.

Pandemonium reigned in the Roman camp. The soldiers were in disarray. Those on duty fought fiercely, but most were unprepared, in their tents, just waking up, in the toilets, in the bath house, preparing their breakfast. They heard the trumpet call to arms and tried to grab their weapons, fumbling as they tried to remove the leather covers from their shields. Hywel drove his chariot through the camp, overturning tents, cutting down the soldiers with the fierce blades on the chariot wheels, swinging his huge two-handed sword.

Llwyd was with Ceiriog and the horsemen. He snorted, twisting and turning, head up, ears alert. Suddenly, he reared on his hind legs, and let out a huge neighing. He made off at a canter in the direction of the pack animals with Ceiriog and the other horses in pursuit. They rode like the wind through the Roman soldiers, riding along the side of the horse or even under the belly, avoiding the spears, or any other missiles thrown at them by the Romans, cutting down all who stood in their path, until they pulled up in front of where Rhiannon and Caradog lay bound.

Rhiannon said later that what happened next seemed like a strange dream. She looked up and saw Llwyd. Stumbling to her feet, she leapt onto his back. Feeling the warmth and comfort of his body once more gave her renewed strength. She grabbed the reins. Hywel's chariot swung into her view, he jumped down and with many helping hands, he lifted Caradog into the vehicle. Horses and chariot turned, and Hywel, riding like a demon back through the enemy, swept towards the gate. The chariots, horsemen and warriors thundered through the gates, into the forest and up the hillside, leaving the Roman camp in utter devastation.

Smoke and fire had destroyed many of the tents. Animals' frightened sounds could be heard as they tried to escape the flames, carts were turned over. Many Romans and Silurians lay wounded or slain. Lepidus was dead. So were Hilarion, and Suetonius. Rhidian had been pierced in the side by a Roman sword and Gwyn, wounded by a missile thrown by Lepidus just before the tribune died.

VICTORY AND CELEBRATION

The Silurians rejoice at the rescue of their leader and a traitor is punished. Brychan tells a story.

AND SO, Hywel returned to Pengelli with Rhiannon and Caradog. The warriors carried them to their home where Meirion and Branwen waited to take care of their wounds and nurse them back to health.

Bledri stood in front of his leader, head bowed, hands tied behind his back.

'What are we going to do with you?' said Hywel. He glanced at Ceiriog, feeling sad for his friend, knowing that the boy would have to be punished according to the law.

'You must do what you think is right,' said Ceiriog, 'I cannot defend my son's actions, I am ashamed to call him Silurian. He will have to be punished and I hope that he may in time learn the error of his ways.'

'Thank you Ceiriog,' said Hywel.' What we do to Bledri in no way reflects on you, we know that you are a true and loyal Silurian, you have fought for us nobly and bravely. But your son has betrayed us and has to be punished.' He paused and looked very solemn. 'My decree is that he is stripped of his noble birth and reduced to slavery. He will be assigned to Gwyn and Eirlys.'

Bledri cringed. This was worse than he had anticipated. He would have to work for the family of the person he hated most – Brychan.

Hywel turned to the people. 'As soon as Caradog and Rhiannon have been restored to health we will celebrate their return and your courage in rescuing them.'

And so it was, that the Silurians gathered at Cefnllwyd for the sacrifice of thanksgiving. Cefnllwyd, the holy place where the stones remembered a time out of memory, a sacred time, remembering the heroes of the past, ancestors of Rhiannon and Caradog, Meirion and Cynan, and of all the Silurians of Pengelli.

The Druids stood in the Stone Circle, Meirion in the centre. A wild boar had been placed on the altar of sacrifice.

Brychan stood with Rhiannon, watching Meirion, the Druid, father of Gwenllian, as he performed the sacred rites.

He looked around him. His sister, Morwen was close by, with Iorwerth and little Chwerthin.

Brychan loved these occasions. There was a smell of wood burning, and the warmth of the blaze protected the girl and boys from the cool evening breezes. It seemed to him a special time and yet it was no-time. Brychan listened to the weird chanting of the priests. The wind moaning through the trees as they twisted their branches upwards towards dark sky.

On such a night, he mused, Arawn, the King of the Otherworld led Pwyll, Prince of Dyfed, into his Kingdom.

They had killed the wild boar. The druids moved around the stone circle, chanting, their dress, their long hair and beards seemed to become part of the trees and the wind and the sky as they went about the mysterious, sacrificial rites. The people watched from the edge of the wood. They were not allowed to come any nearer to the holy place.

Suddenly the chanting of the priests died away on the breeze. The sacrifice was at an end.

Gwyn and Eirlys began to chatter to each other as they moved back to the camp to join the others in the Great Hall for the feast. Meat roasted on spits and stews bubbled away in large cauldrons. Bards and musicians began to play and sing, and people joined with them in the singing.

Rhiannon laughed as she watched the children dressing up in the warriors' cloaks, dancing and singing.

Victory and Celebration

Everyone was gathered in the Great Hall. Caradog was dressed once more in his leader's dress, Emyr on his right and Hywel on his left, He had his arm round his daughter Rhiannon.

Caradog turned to Brychan. 'You have been a good friend to my daughter and I am grateful. Come and sit next to me.'

He turned to his people. 'Enjoy the food and drink that has been prepared for us in the Great Hall. Cynan, play for us.'

So they ate and drank and sang songs and Cynan played beautiful music and told wonderful tales of long ago, of Caradog, sometimes called Caratacus, and of Gwydion and Lleu and Ceridwen. As the bard plucked the last chord on the strings of his harp, Rhiannon turned to her friend.

'Give us a story Brychan,' she said. 'One to remind us of our good fortune in escaping from Roman hands.'

Brychan thought of all the stories he had learned from Cynan.

'I think there can be only one fitting for this evening,' he replied. 'The story of your namesake, an equally beautiful and courageous young woman.'

Rhiannon flushed with pleasure while the people settled themselves comfortably to listen to Brychan's tale. He had already gained a reputation for his gift of story telling.

And so, Brychan told them the story of Rhiannon and how she tricked Gwawl, who wanted to wed her, and how Pwyll whom she loved was guided by her wisdom.

The company were silent as Brychan ended his story. After an evening of good food and wine, music, and Brychan's story, everyone felt contented.

It had been a wonderful celebration of the safe return of Rhiannon and Caradog.

Rhiannon looked across at her friend, her face flushed as she said, 'Thank you Brychan, that was a wonderful tale of a beautiful and wise lady. I can never live up to her reputation, but I am glad I bear her name.'

Victory and Celebration

Then Caradog stood up and looked around at the gathering.

'We have enjoyed a splendid celebration tonight and heard a wonderful tale from Brychan. I think he is one of your star pupils, Cynan.'

Cynan smiled and the people applauded Brychan once more.

Rhiannon and Brychan left the Great Hall and wandered out into the night. They stood on the brow of the hill looking out towards the Great Water. Rhiannon did not need to look in her mirror. She watched the Roman ships in the distance sailing once more towards the shores of her land.

She sighed. 'Tell me another story Brychan.' she said.

THE STORY OF RHIANNON FROM THE MABINOGION

(as told by Brychan in the Great Hall at Pengelli)

'YOU know that the goddess Rhiannon was as wise as she was beautiful. And you know how Pwyll pursued her as, dressed in a garment of shining gold, she rode by on a pure white horse. You know that he failed to catch her however fast he rode, although she seemed always to ride slowly. And you know that he finally learned wisely that he only had to ask her to and she immediately waited for him. He learned that she loved him greatly and was happy to agree to his request. You also know that they arranged to celebrate their wedding at her home with her father, Hefydd the Old. It is this story that I want to tell you. A story of the foolishness of Pwyll, the wickedness of Gwawl, and the wisdom of Rhiannon.

'It all began at the home of Hefydd the Old and his daughter, Rhiannon. Those of you who know the story will remember how Pwyll first saw Rhiannon, wearing her cloth of gold and riding her pure white horse. You will remember how he immediately fell in love with her, and how she promised to marry him a year from that day.

"Come to my home," she said, "we will have great feasting and rejoicing, and we will be married."

"Gladly," agreed Pwyll, for she was the most beautiful woman he had ever seen and he loved her with all his heart.

'And so it fell out. Pwyll travelled to Rhiannon's home with all his warriors, and many of his friends. They arrived at the home of Hefydd the Old and were made welcome by father and daughter. A great feast was prepared and Pwyll sat at the high table with Rhiannon on his right and Hefydd on his left. She wore her beautiful dress of silk gold, a gold bracelet twined itself round her smooth white arm, and a cunningly carved torc was clasped round her long white neck. Her thickly braided gold tresses hung heavily down her back. Pwyll looked at his bride and his heart filled with joy at the prospect of being wed to such a wise and beautiful princess.

'As they feasted and talked together, music and laughter filled the hall, then, something made Pwyll look up and he saw a tall auburn-haired youth, dressed in garments of gold and silk approaching his table. He was a stranger, and Pwyll greeted him politely.

"Come and sit down. Although I do not recognise you, on such a happy occasion, all are welcome here, especially outsiders."

"I am no stranger to these parts," said the youth, "and I come to beg a favour from you."

'Pwyll, flushed with happiness, and with the good food and wine, said carelessly, "This day, I have been so blessed by the gods, I wish to share my happiness with others. I will grant you whatever you wish for."

As he uttered these words, Rhiannon looked both sad and angry.

"Why did you speak so rashly?" she cried.

'The strange youth continued, "The lady whom I love above all other is the lady who is to be your bride. I come to ask you to give her to me."

Pwyll sat stunned and silent.

"Be silent as long as you like," said Rhiannon, angrily, "no man ever spoke so foolishly as you have done."

"My heart," said Pwyll, "I did not know who he was!"

"He is the man to whom I was to be given against my will," she said. "He is Gwawl, son of Clud. And you cannot go back on your given word."

"I cannot do it," said Pwyll wretchedly.

"You must. Do it," said Rhiannon, "and I will bring it about that I shall never be his."

"How will you do that?" said Pwyll with amazement.

"I will give you a small bag," she said. "Keep it well. I will promise to be his bride in a year's time. At the end of the year, see that you attend the ceremony, and bring the bag with you. Hide your warriors in the hills behind. When he is in the midst of joy and feasting, come into the hall dressed in rags, wearing large clumsy old shoes and holding the bag in your hand. Ask for nothing but a bag of food. However much food is put into it, I will make sure that the bag is never full. Gwawl will become impatient and ask if the bag will ever be full. You must then say that it will never be full until a man of noble birth and great wealth presses down the food inside the bag with both his feet, saying there is enough food in this bag. As soon as he puts his feet into the bag, you must quickly pull the bag over his head and tie it tightly. Make sure you have a good horn around your neck and sound it at that time to summon your warriors from the hills. When they hear the sound of the horn, they will come down and seize Gwawl's men and cast them into prison."

'And so it came about. Gwawl returned to his land, and Pwyll returned to Dyfed.

'When a year had passed, Gwawl, son of Clud, set out for Rhiannon's home. He was received there with feasting and rejoicing, as Rhiannon had promised. Pwyll also did as Rhiannon had bid him. He journeyed to Rhiannon's home with his warriors, who then hid in the hills behind the Great Hall. Pwyll dressed in rags and carrying the bag given to him by Rhiannon, and wearing large clumsy old shoes on his feet, went into the hall and saluted Gwawl and his company.

"Blessings upon you," said Gwawl, "you are welcome here, ask of me anything which I think is just and I will grant it to you."

"All I crave is food," said Pwyll, "for I am very hungry. If you would but fill this small bag with meat, I would be grateful."

"That is a reasonable request, and there is more than enough food here for all, especially for the poor and hungry. Bring him food," Gwawl commanded.

So his servants hurried forward to fill the bag held out by Pwyll. But however much food they pressed into the bag it never seemed full! At last, Gwawl exclaimed, "This is very strange! We keep filling your bag but the food never seems to appear at the surface. Will your bag never be full?"

"It will not," declared Pwyll, "unless a man of wealth and nobility himself rises and presses down the food with both his feet. As he does so, he must say 'enough has been put therein.' Only then will the bag be full and my request be honourably satisfied."

'Then Rhiannon said to Gwawl, "Rise up quickly, or your command will never be met and your honour satisfied."

"Willingly," said Gwawl. He immediately rose and placed both his feet in the bag to press down the food as he had been advised. No sooner had he done so than Pwyll quickly pulled the bag over his head and tied the thongs tightly so that he could not escape. At the same time he blew his horn and his warriors rode down from the hills and seized the men of Gwawl by surprise, and carried them off to prison. So Gwawl was trapped and helpless.

'Pwyll threw off his tattered rags and his clumsy old shoes and appeared in his princely garments once more. Meanwhile, his warriors amused themselves by beating on the bag in which Gwawl was trapped until he was sorely bruised.

As his tormentors continued to beat him. Gwawl's voice could be heard from within the recesses of the bag. "If you would listen, I beg you not to allow me to be slain, lying here as I do, defeated and helpless."

Hefydd the Old said, "I think he should be heard, no-one deserves such punishment."

"I will do as Rhiannon advises me," said Pwyll.

"Then I advise you to make him promise never to seek revenge for that which has been done to him, that will be punishment enough," said Rhiannon.

"I will promise this gladly," said Gwawl.

"And I will gladly accept your promise," said Pwyll, "since it is the counsel of Hefydd and Rhiannon."

"And I will stand as his surety, that he will not break his promise," said Hefydd

'With that Gwawl was let out of the bag and his warriors were set free.

"Let me go to anoint my bruises," said Gwawl, "for I am very sore."

'So Pwyll gave him permission to leave the hall. And then, he and Rhiannon and all the company feasted and rejoiced in celebration of the marriage of Pwyll and Rhiannon. All spent the night in mirth and merriment, but happiest of all were Pwyll, Prince of Dyfed and his wise and beautiful bride Rhiannon.'

PRONUNCIATION OF THE NAMES OF LOCATIONS AND CHARACTERS

Pengelli	(*Penn-**ge**-ll-ee*)	Delwyn	(***Del**-Winn*)
Brynpwca	(*Brin-**poo**-ka*)	Ehedydd	(*Eh-**head**-dith*)
		Arianwen	(*Arr-ee-**an**-wen*)
Caradog	(*Car-**rad**-dog*)	Rhodri	(*Rh-**od**-ree*)
Branwen	(***Bran**-wen*)	Rhys	(*Rh-**ees***)
Rhiannon	(*Rh-ee-**yann**-on*)	Pryderi	(*Prud-**derree***)
Gweneira	(*Gwen-**ay**-ra*)	Chwerthin	(*Ch-**werr**-thin*)
Owain	(***Owe**-wine*)	Gwyn	(*G-winn*)
Penarddun	(*Pen-**arr**-theen*)	Eirlys	(***Ay**-rr-lis*)
Bryn	(*Brinn*)	Brychan	(***Bru**-ch-an* – with the Bru as in "Brush")
Hywel	(***How**-el*)		
Gwenllian	(***Gwen**-ll-ee-yan*)		
Iorwerth	(*Yorr – **werr** – th*)	Morwen	(***Morr**-wen*)
Eleri	(*El-**air**-ee*)	Cynan	(***Cunn**-an*)
Euros	(***Ay** – ros*)	Aurwen	(***Ay**-rr-wen*)
Meirion	(***May**-ree-yon*)	Arianrhod	(*Arr-ee-**yan**-rh-od*)
Rhidian	(*Rrh-**id**-yan*)	Cenwyn	(***Ken**-winn*)
Cigfa	(***Kig**-fa*)	Ceiriog	(***Cay**-ree-og*)
Emyr	(***Em**-eer*)	Llun	(*Ll-**ee**-n*)
Collen	(***Co**-ll-en*)	Bledri	(***Bled**-ree*)
Heulwen	(***Hayl**-wen*)	Bradach	(***Brad**-ah-ch*)

For "ll" Put your tongue into the right position to say L, and then blow hard.

Rh is pronounced similar to r but you should hear the "h".

The "dd" said as in the "th" of "that".

Ch is pronounced softly at the back of the throat - as in the Scottish word "Loch".

THE SILURIANS AT PENGELLI

Caradog's House
Caradog, Silurian leader (aged 28)
Branwen, his wife (aged 26)
Rhiannon, daughter (aged 12)
Gweneira, daughter (aged 8)
Owain, son (aged 3)
Penarddun, Caradog's mother (aged 45)
Bryn, Branwen's father (aged 43)

Hywel's House
Hywel, Caradog's brother (aged 27)
Gwenllian, his wife (aged 24)
Iorwerth, son (aged 8)
Eleri, daughter (aged 6)
Euros, son (aged 3)
Meirion, the Druid, Gwenllian's father (42)

Rhidian's House
Rhidian, the Smith, Caradog's brother (aged 22)
Cigfa, his wife (aged 21)

Arianwen's House
Arianwen, Caradog's sister (aged 20)
Rhodri, her husband (aged 21)
Rhys, son (aged 6)
Pryderi, son (aged 3)
Chwerthin, daughter (aged 2)

Gwyn's House
Gwyn, Brychan's father (aged 28)
Eirlys, Brychan's, mother (aged 26)
Brychan (aged 12)
Morwen, Brychan's sister (aged 10)

Cynan's House
Cynan, the chief Bard (aged 35)
Aurwen, his wife (aged 30)
Arianrhod, daughter (aged 13)
Cenwyn, son (aged 12)

Ceirog's House
Ceiriog, Bledri's father (aged 28)
Llun, Bledri's mother (aged 26)
Bledri (aged 12)

Emyr's House
Emyr, Branwen's brother (aged 26)
Collen, his wife (aged 24)
Heulwen, daughter (aged 8)
Delwyn, son (aged 6)
Ehedydd, daughter (aged 3)

THE ROMANS AT BRYNPWCA

Legate: Aulus Maximus Ostorius (aged 38)
Tribune: Cassius Ligarius Lepidus (aged 24)
Centurion: Marcus Quintus Lutorius (aged 25)
Optio: Suetonius Claudius Tullus (aged 22)

Roman soldiers:
(in the story)

Quintus Publius Aemilius (aged 20)
Gaius Octavius Varro (aged 21)
Flavius Hilarion Paulus (aged 19)
Varrius Germanicus Messala (aged 18)
Taurus Drusillus Cato (aged 17)

Auxiliary soldiers:
in the story:

Esca, a Celt from Gaul, (aged 16)
Bradach, a Celt from Brittany, (aged 16)

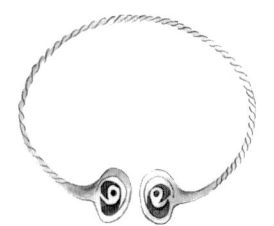

Cynan (35) m Aurwen (30)
- Arianrhod (13)
- Cenwyn (12)

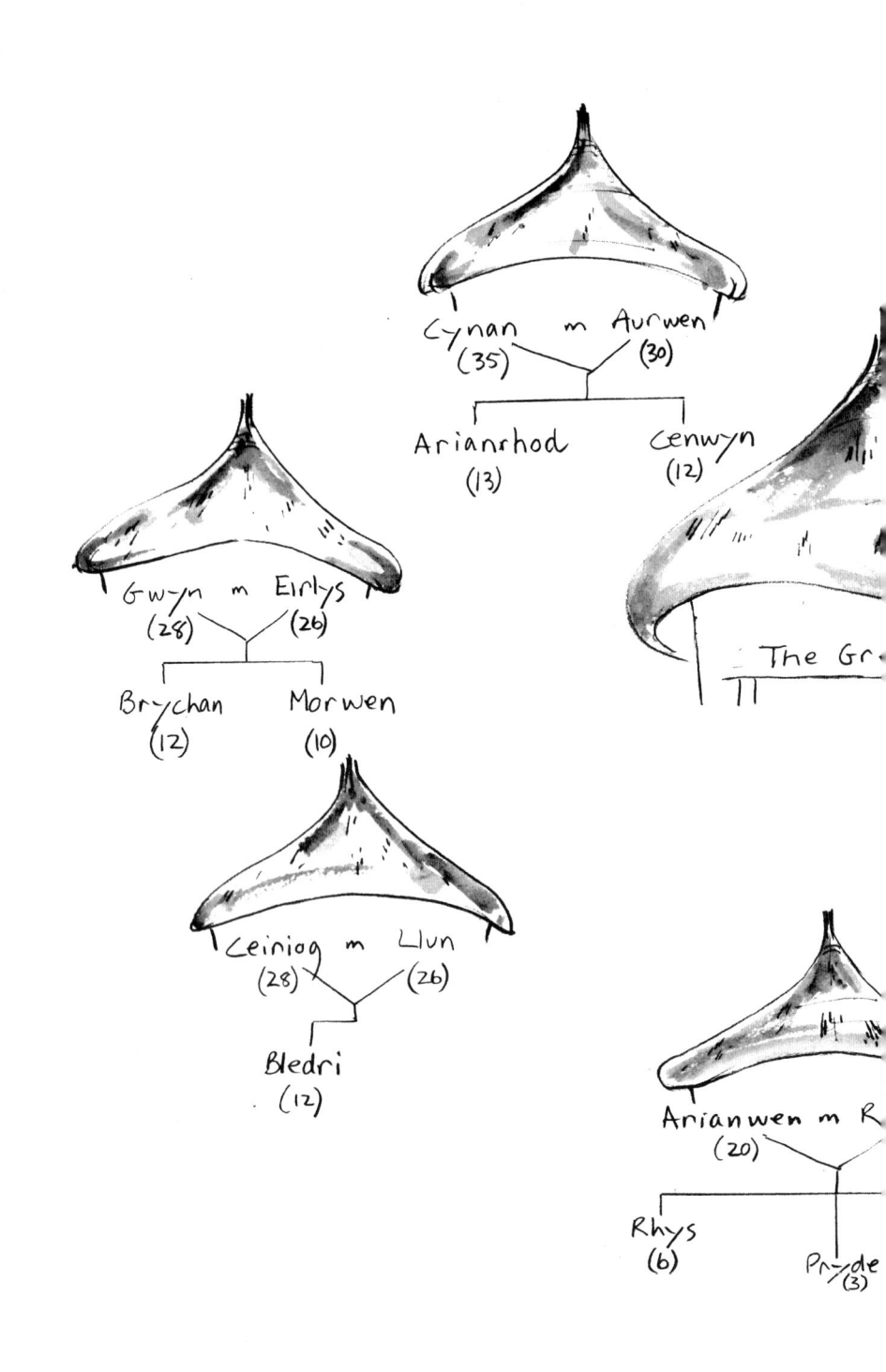

Gwyn (28) m Eirlys (26)
- Brychan (12)
- Morwen (10)

Ceiniog (28) m Llun (26)
- Bledri (12)

The Gr...

Arianwen (20) m R...
- Rhys (6)
- Pr...de (3)